V L KNIGHT

The Blackstone Bargain - V L Knight

The Northern Grit & Gown Series: Book One

T. James
Paws&Print.

First published by T. James, Paws&Print.
https://tjamespawsprint.co.uk Contact:
hello@tjamespawsprint.co.uk 2025

First edition

ISBN: 978-1-9191914-0-9

This book was professionally typeset on Reedsy.
Find out more at reedsy.com

For my mum,
who gave me stories, and the encouragement to write my own.

And for my children,
may you never settle for less than everything.

Upon Yorkshire's windswept moors they stand,
Where regency whispers through heathered land.
Florence Ashcroft, with grit in her eyes,
Seeks honour 'midst bargains and truth from the lies.

Lord Blackstone guards wealth in his ancient estate,
Yet love blooms quietly beyond fortune's gate.
"Be reyt," says the earth beneath boots worn and true—
In rot or in riches, hearts find their due.

-UNKNOWN

Foreword

Welcome to Regency Yorkshire, where soot clings to stone, industry hums just beyond the manor gates, and reputations can be shattered by a single kiss. The Blackstone Bargain is set not in the ballrooms of Mayfair, but in the shifting landscapes of the North, where old money clashes with new enterprise, scandal hides in fog, and love must fight its way through pride, grief, and gossip. It's a story of bargains and consequences. Of a woman with too much to lose, and a man already ruined. Of factory smoke, family legacies, supper menus, bonfires, and longing so tightly restrained it could ignite at a touch. Florence Ashcroft runs half a valley and has no intention of giving that up for marriage. Elias Blackstone would rather rot in his ancestral hall than ask for help. Naturally, they're forced together. I hope you fall for them the way I did, slowly, stubbornly, and all at once.

V.L. Knight

Preface

I've always been in love with stories. As a girl, I read under the covers long past bedtime, candlelight in spirit, torchlight in practice. Historical romance, in particular, cast its spell early. There's something irresistible about corsets and consequences, brooding men who pretend they feel nothing, and women clever enough to call their bluff. This book was written in the margins of my life between work, parenting teenagers, feeding cats, and stealing moments of peace between coffee and wine. I wrote when I was tired, when I doubted myself, and when my cats helpfully stepped across my keyboard to add their own edits. I wrote through plot holes and school runs and that maddening final round of edits where nothing is ever quite finished. And still I kept going. The Blackstone Bargain is a love letter to slow burns, sharp heroines, brooding Yorkshire lords, and the authors who inspired me: Elizabeth Gaskell, Jane Austen, and the Brontes. Their stories taught me that love is rarely tidy, never convenient, and almost always arrives at the worst possible time. I hope this book gives you what I always look for in a good romance: escape, tension, tenderness and the thrill of two people discovering that love, when it finally comes, is worth every risk.

Now then, shall we?

Acknowledgments

A Gracious nod to T. James Paws&Print for sponsoring this literary endeavour with both ISBNs and paternal pride. Your patronage shall be remembered in the annals of publishing… and the family WhatsApp chat.

A Note from Lord Blackstone

To the discerning reader, this novel adheres to **British English spelling and grammar**, befitting its setting, its author, and, if I may be so bold, its narrator. You may notice the presence of honour with a u, realise with an s, and the occasional reference to trousers rather than pants. I assure you, none of these are errors. Should any unfamiliar words appear, I trust you'll rise to the challenge. After all, what's a little linguistic variety between friends? Now then, if we're quite finished with orthography, I believe we have business to attend to.

-Lord Blackstone

Prologue

Mooredge Hall, Yorkshire. Winter 1803.

Elias stood at the edge of the frozen lawn, collar stiff against the wind. He watched the black-clad figures drift inside as though nothing had happened. The church bell had long since stopped tolling, but its echo still rang in his ears.

Behind him, Mooredge Hall loomed dark and silent, holding its breath now that its master lay in the ground. He hadn't cried at the graveside or through the endless condolences pressed into his hands by people who'd never looked him in the eye before today.

His father had not been a kind man. Nor cruel, exactly. Just... absent.

Even when he was present, his father told him. "Learn to keep your shoulders back and your mouth shut, and everything else will follow." Then he'd gone back to his letters. That was as close to a blessing as he had ever given him. So Elias had kept his shoulders back and shut his mouth. And still, there was nothing—no sense of peace. No clarity. Simply wind, silence and a name that now belonged to him, whether he wanted it or not.

His mother's heeled boots clicked on the flagstones behind him. He didn't turn, but he knew it was her by the faint scent of lavender laced with the bitter note of wine beneath it. "Elias," she said, her voice smooth and dry. "Don't sulk. It doesn't suit you."

"I'm not sulking," he muttered.

"Mm, brooding then. Very becoming." She came to stand beside him; her gloved hand sliding into the crook of his arm, not affectionately, but as though she simply expected it there.

He glanced at her. Her eyes glinted in the weak winter light, watching the house.

"You don't intend to stay," he said flatly.

"Of course not. I've endured enough years in this mausoleum. I don't intend to finish my life in Yorkshire playing at the grieving widow. And nor should you, not at sixteen."

"Where, then?"

"London. I've already written to Robert."

Robert Delling. Viscount Cheverley. The man who'd been at their table so many evenings, Elias could no longer remember when it had begun. "He'll marry you?"

His mother's mouth curved into a faint smile. "Don't be obtuse, darling. He's not marrying me for love."

No, Elias thought, no one married for love. But Robert cared for her in his own quiet, stubborn way. And for Elias, too, though neither of them would have called it that aloud.

Elias remembered how Robert had pressed a hand to his shoulder the first night he arrived in London, a brief wordless promise.

He exhaled, his breath white in the cold air.

"We'll leave tomorrow," his mother said briskly.

Elias frowned. "I want to say goodbye to the house."

That earned him a rare, amused glance. "You really are your father's son."

She walked back toward the Hall. He stayed, staring up at

the silent windows, waiting for some flicker of warmth that never came.

If this was what love looked like, silence, duty, bargains struck in the dark, he wanted no part of it.

1

Chapter One

Mooredge Hall, Yorkshire, early September, 1814

The carriage lurched through another rut, its wheels groaning under the weight of mud thick as treacle. Beyond the mist-clouded windows, the bleak moorland stretched in every direction, wind-scoured and unrepentant. Far off, skeletal trees clawed at the sky, and smoke from Calderbank's mills blurred the horizon into a smear of soot and industry, as if God himself had tried to wipe the land clean and given up.

Elias Blackstone sat in still silence, save for the steady tap of one black-gloved finger against his knee with each jolt. His dark hair was unfashionably severe, swept back with careless precision. His clothes were tailored but austere, whispering of old money and older grudges. Nothing about him begged for attention, and yet, it rarely strayed far.

"Nearly there, my lord," came the muffled voice of the coachman. "Should see the Hall any moment now."

Elias didn't look. He remembered it. Mooredge Hall had loomed through his boyhood like a monument to things he'd never quite earned: pride, legacy, approval. And now he returned, not as its son, but as its master. Wealthy enough to reclaim it, disgraced enough to need it. His reputation had collapsed in Mayfair faster than a chimney stack on the west wing, and he wasn't sure which left more debris.

Across from him sat his mother, Lady Cheverley, who adjusted the cuffs of her gloves with meticulous distaste. Still striking in her widow's finery, she remained composed and immaculately distant. London's salons had once adored her, and she them. But London had a short memory and longer knives.

She broke the silence with a sigh sharp enough to draw blood. "You'll find the air bracing," she said, green eyes fixed on the window's condensation. "Or suffocating, depending on how long one intends to remain in exile."

Elias exhaled. "Let's hope the locals favour silence over speculation."

She raised a brow. "Darling. This is Yorkshire. They'll *speculate in verse* if you give them the chance."

The house emerged through the fog, three storeys of Yorkshire grit and architectural disappointment. Ivy clung to its greying sandstone like old transgressions rising to the roof.

The carriage creaked to a stop, and Elias stepped out before the footman could reach the door. The wind hit him hard, thick with coal dust, rain, and memory. He scanned the grounds. Dying hedges. Sagging stables. A knot of servants gathered on the steps, stiff with curiosity.

London had chewed up the Blackstones and spat them out scandal-stained and silent. Now here they were again, titled, tarnished, and dragging their sins back to the Yorkshire soil that remembered *everything*.

"Tha's 'im then, is it?" muttered a stableboy.

"Aye. Looks broody, don't he?"

"Course he does," dry as soot. "Them what come from dishonour always do."

Elias said nothing. If they thought the accent made their words harmless, they'd forgotten one thing: Yorkshire was still his. He'd bled on these stones.

Lady Cheverley descended with deliberate grace. The carriage door may as well have been her stage curtain. She emerged tall and composed, wearing grey skirts trimmed in black lace, her veil sheer enough to catch a glimpse of the cold curve of her smile.

An officious-looking woman, whose uniform was immaculately pressed, stepped from the threshold and curtsied low.

"Lord Blackstone. Lady Cheverley. Welcome home." Her voice was clipped, with no trace of a Yorkshire burr. Crisp vowels and careful posture. This must be Mrs Vale, the newly appointed housekeeper.

Elias inclined his head and mounted the steps; he moved like a man long practised at holding his breath, grief, and opinions.

Home. The word ought to have stirred something, bitterness, perhaps, or memory. But he felt nothing.

He hadn't wanted to return. And if the rumours had arrived before him, so be it. Let them talk. Let the whole county recall, if they must, the night London's drawing rooms fell silent over the duel.

How Lord Norbury had cornered Lady Cheverley in a moment meant for ruin. And how Elias had intervened. Bloodied his gloves. Burned his reputation to keep hers intact.

He was no longer the darling of the season. No blushing debutante would ever risk herself on a man whispered to have gone feral over family honour. Not when better titles came unsoiled.

But Mooredge? Mooredge didn't care. The hall had stood long before Elias Blackstone was born, and before his mother ever wore the name. It had seen worse than him. And it would surely see worse again.

The vast entrance hall was colder than outside. Damp stone struck him first, mingled with long-dead fires and something metallic beneath the varnish of age. The rugs were threadbare. Mirrors clouded. A chandelier loomed above, all dust and lost grandeur, like a frozen storm threatening to fall.

Lady Cheverley removed her gloves one finger at a time. "Well. Either that's mildew or the soul of your great-grandfather's ambition."

Elias didn't answer. He crossed the flagstones, each step echoing like an accusation. Everything remained exactly as he remembered. What had once seemed monumental now stood reduced to its true, shrunken scale. Once, he'd thought the house alive. Now it was tired. Just like him.

Footsteps echoed behind him, more servants, more murmurs. They kept a cautious distance, eyes flicking to his boots, his coat, and his silence. Not one had followed from London. No servant worth their starch would trade the city for wind-chapped moors and a tarnished name. Even his valet had invented an ailing aunt and practically leapt at the chance to stay behind. So here he stood, in a house that remembered him as a boy, and made no secret of its disappointment.

"This way, my lord, my lady," said Mrs Vale, leading them toward the staircase, her expression unreadable. She had the poise of someone accustomed to filling the space between absence and disappointment.

"I give it six months," Lady Cheverley murmured as they climbed the ancient staircase.

"Six months for what?" he asked.

"For you to curse every decision that brought you here," his mother replied, "but you'll curse it with dignity, which is something."

He didn't answer; he agreed, but didn't wish to give his mother the satisfaction.

The walls bore gaps where paintings had once hung. One had been a hunting scene, all blood and pride. Another, his grandfather's portrait, a grim man with the eyes of a hawk and a mouth built for disapproval. It had terrified him as a child. Now, its absence unsettled him more.

At the end of the corridor, past shuttered guest chambers and a nursery gone to dust, he found the master's suite. Elias paused at the door. His hand hesitated at the latch, as if the ghost of his father might still pace within, reciting ledgers and legacy like scripture.

Muslin sheets veiled the room's windows, filtering light to a sickly grey. The hearth lay bare, its grate black with ancient ash. Dust clung to the furniture, not thick enough to forget, but enough to suggest no one had dared disturb it.

His father's presence had made this chamber vast. In his absence, it was more like a shrine than a seat of power.

When he was twelve, and leaving for school, his father had summoned him, a rare and weighty honour. Elias had stood straighter, hoping for something like pride, something warm he could carry with him. Instead, he received instructions—brisk, bloodless, and offered with all the warmth of an invoice.

"One day, all this will be yours," his father said, gaze fixed somewhere beyond him. More of an order than a promise. Elias had nodded, trying not to look disappointed. Trying to earn what would never be given. He'd been naïve then. Hungry for approval. He used to draw maps of the estate on the backs of his Latin translations—adding footpaths, marking new wells, planning gardens where none had ever grown. He dreamt of lighting fires in every hearth, of cutting back the choking vines to let in the light, restoration as redemption. Foolish.

He dragged the sheet from the armchair nearest the hearth and dropped onto it without ceremony. Dust plumed around him like a protest.

Yorkshire. Bloody Yorkshire. His mother wished him to re-enter society's little theatre. Smile, dance, charm some well-bred daughter with lineage enough to launder his name.

Even with funds to spare, they'd barely have the infrastructure to heat this place, let alone host. Wealth couldn't conjure warmth from crumbling walls. Still. What else could he do?

He stared at the empty grate, fingers tightening on the chair arms. Mooredge Hall deserved better than decay. Maybe he did too. He scrubbed a hand over his face.

He didn't know how to be this man, the one who fought for honour and came out with a name in ashes and an estate full of ghosts. But he would learn.

He always had.

2

Chapter Two

Dinner was… brown.

That was Elias's first observation as he glared at the plate set before him. Brown meat, brown gravy, and brown pudding of uncertain origin. And something beige that steamed faintly, as though trying to disguise its intentions.

He blinked once. "Is this—?"

"It's proper, that is," the maid declared, beaming like she'd presented a royal feast. "Potted beef wi' suet crust. Bit o' dripping toast. Pudding's black, mind—we've none of that white gentry sauce you're likely used to."

"Right," Elias said, eyeing his knife like it might somehow solve the situation. "Of course."

The girl darted off before he could ask her anything further.

At the far end of the long, candlelit table, Lady Cheverley sipped her red wine with detached grace. She'd changed into black lace over dove-grey silk and had coiled her dark hair in a style that no Yorkshire maid could have achieved without divine intervention.

"This is authentic," Elias muttered, nudging the crust with

his fork.

His mother didn't look up. "It's edible. Which I suspect is the full extent of culinary ambition here."

He prodded the meat. "We'll need a better cook."

"We'll need several things, darling. A cook, a valet, and carpet not infested with silverfish."

Mooredge's dining room, like the rest of the house, had not aged gracefully. The ceiling hadn't fallen, though it looked as though it once considered it. No grandeur remained, only blistered paint, and the memory of fire. The candles cast long, narrow shadows, as if the walls were stretching away from them. Behind his mother, a faded tapestry sagged on its hooks—depicting, Elias thought, either a hunting party or the martyrdom of Saint Hubert. Possibly both.

"It's smaller than I remember," she said eventually.

"You always preferred London's scale," he said dryly.

She tilted her head. "It needs more than a coat of paint." Her eyes flicked over to him. "And so do you."

He exhaled, slow and measured. "It is a temporary arrangement. I shall oversee the repairs, restore what can be salvaged, and play the dutiful heir if that is what decency requires. And then, Mother, I shall return to London with a suitable wife and a cleansed reputation."

"Suitable?" Her lips twitched. "You'll have to lower your standards."

"I already have."

That earned him a small smile. "Well. You've always had taste. Just not sense."

He didn't rise to the bait. This wasn't defeat. It was *penance*. And if he played his part to perfection, it might yet bring the redemption he once sought.

She set her wine down and said almost idly, "I had a maid go up to the attic."

Elias glanced up. "Have you already taken up ghost hunting?"

"There's furniture up there," she continued, unfazed. "Paintings. Trunks covered in dust, naturally, but there's history in it. Some of it is fine. Possibly even valuable."

He straightened. "Truly?"

She gave a regal nod. "Old Blackstone pieces. Portraits. A grandfather clock that doesn't chime, a harp missing half its strings—but yes. The bones are here. What you restore is up to you."

Before he could reply, Mrs Vale appeared in the doorway like a well-schooled spectre, holding a ledger and her composure.

"My lord," she said, inclining her head. "If I may. The inventory is lacking. Disrepair is evident in the servants' quarters. The stables are functional, in the loosest sense. And the roof above the west wing leaks. Badly."

"And the good news, Mrs Vale?" he said.

"We've not yet succumbed to pestilence," she said blankly.

Lady Cheverley gave a bark of laughter.

Elias held out his hand for the ledger. "Let me see."

Mrs Vale didn't hand it over. "I'll summarise. Apparitions and good intentions cannot make the Hall comfortable again. I'll need permission to hire."

"You have it," Elias said quickly. His fingers twitching restlessly. "Do what's necessary."

She nodded once, crisp as a page turn. "There's a boy in the village. Smart. Respectable family. Could serve as your valet."

"A valet? From Rookhaven?" he said, brow wrinkling.

Her mouth pinched. "Not everyone in Yorkshire is livestock, my lord."

His mother sipped her wine. "Though some do chew cud at dinner."

Elias ignored them both. "Fine. Send for him. And for God's sake, have someone look at the chimney in the study. It sounds like it's trying to eat the wind." Elias sighed. "And the stables, *functional?*" he added, rubbing at his temple. "Christ. I went out before dinner. The roof's gone in on one corner, half the tack is mouldering, and the head groom is either half-blind or wholly drunk."

His mother set down her glass with a soft clink. "Fortunately, we're surrounded by more stone and brick than even your pride can resist. You'll restore it."

He leaned back, eyes on the blackened beams overhead. The house was broken, bruised by time and neglect. But it endured. And for now, so must he.

* * *

Elias woke with a crick in his neck and the taste of dust on his tongue. Pale light bled through the muslin-draped windows, staining the stone floor the colour of old bone.

He was still in his coat and boots. His cravat hung loose at his throat, and one glove lay on the rug like a forgotten relic. He hadn't undressed. He couldn't.

His father's bed was stiff with age, the sheets coarse and stained in places the candlelight hadn't revealed. The thought of lying beneath them had made his skin crawl. There were some ghosts; one did not sleep beside.

He sat up, brushing cobwebs from his sleeve. The air was even bleaker than the night before, the kind of cold that didn't just settle in the bones, but questioned whether one deserved warmth at all.

Furniture slouched beneath dust cloths like creatures in hibernation. The wardrobe stood ajar, its single hook empty. The bedchamber still smelled of wax, but beneath it, something else. Something like regret, steeped into the stones. He crossed to the window. Mooredge's grounds stretched below. His reflection stared back—hollow-eyed and unshaven.

London had cast him out. Yorkshire hadn't exactly welcomed him back—polite smiles, cautious glances—but no, not welcomed. Perhaps not ever.

The memory surfaced like a bruise pressed too hard: Norbury's hand on his mother's wrist. Too familiar. Too possessive. That *filthy smile.* The scent of overripe roses, the stifling heat of too many candles in a Mayfair drawing room, and the hum of too many mouths pretending not to watch. Then his words—poison, meant for the room as much as her.

"If you're bored with playing mother, darling, I'm happy to let you play whore instead."

Her laugh faltered. Her breath caught. And Elias… didn't think. His fist landed before his mind caught up—bone on bone, loud enough to silence the room. Norbury staggered, bloodied and grinning.

"Dawn, then," the man had said, throwing down his gloves.

"Dawn," Elias answered, without hesitation.

It hadn't been planned. But it had been inevitable. A summer morning. Grey sky, dew-slicked grass, air heavy with the threat of rain.

"You don't have to kill him."

Norbury had wanted a spectacle. And Elias—God help him—had given it to him.

One shot clean through Norbury's shoulder. One breath where all of Mayfair seemed to hold its tongue. Then the whispers. The retreat. The stain. Norbury had bled. Elias had stayed standing. And his future had started to rot.

Within days, his name was everywhere—but never spoken aloud. At White's, Elias's name was struck from the books. Brooks sent word that his subscription was no longer welcome. At the fencing rooms, benches filled, sparring partners, and invitations vanished. The name *Lord Blackstone* now came with a sneer.

His mother didn't speak of it. She simply packed her trunks and adopted the face of dignified suffering.

She'd always hunted for safety. And he, fool that he was, had tried to give it to her.

He closed his eyes. His father had taught him not to cry. Robert Delling, Viscount Cheverley, had at least taught him how to hold his ground. A man of quiet decency, who'd left Elias a fortune with one condition: *Look after your mother.*

Of course, he would, but no one warned him what protecting *her* would cost.

3

Chapter Three

The breakfast parlour smelled of onions.

Elias peered at the spread laid before him with dread. Something unidentifiable shimmered with grease under the grey morning light. A teapot sat cooling by his elbow, flanked by a slab of yellow cheese, oatcakes, and what might have been an egg, though it bore closer resemblance to a dare.

He cleared his throat. "Is this breakfast, or have I been misled entirely?"

The parlour maid grinned, pleased with the kitchen's efforts. "That there's bacon collar, m'lord. And black puddin' wi' tatie cakes. Proper start to the day."

"Hmm," Elias muttered, lifting his fork like a man going into battle. "Where is the cook?"

"In the kitchen, I reckon."

"I'd like a word with her."

Ten minutes later, Elias found himself in the cavernous, grease-stained kitchen facing a woman of indeterminate age with arms like bread loaves and a bun so tightly coiled it looked liable to snap a man's resolve.

She gave him a brisk curtsey, wiping her hands on her apron. "Mornin' yer lordship. I'm Maud. Head cook. What's the matter wi' breakfast, then? Too crisp? Too soft? Or just not London enough?"

Elias blinked. "Pardon?"

"I said," she repeated, with the calm efficiency of a woman who'd buried at least one husband, "was it too crisp or too soft or not fancy enough for a gent like you? Cause I done it proper, like my mam taught me. I cooked at the Spotted Hen for twelve year, and no bugger ever spat nowt back."

He held up a hand. "No, no, I'm sure it's genuine. It's… not quite what I'm accustomed to."

"Soft bellies in London," Maud sniffed. "Eat nowt, but air and ideas."

"Could you possibly prepare something simpler? Toast. Eggs. Maybe coffee that doesn't glower?"

She squinted at him. "I'll see what I can manage. But you'll not get fancy French beans nor them watered-down milk tricks. And you'd shatter in a stiff wind if I fed you nowt but what you're used to."

"Fine," Elias muttered. "We'll fight that battle another day."

She beamed. "Aye. You will."

* * *

Elias crossed the weed-choked drive, boots crunching over gravel that had seen better centuries. Mist clung to the edges of the fields, and the old stone wall marking the boundary of the estate sagged like a drunkard in prayer. Nearby, a rooster crowed in open defiance of its surroundings.

He found the groundsman at the far gate, hammering at a bent hinge with the sort of determination that suggested the tool had wronged him. “You’re the head groundsman, then?” Elias called.

The man looked up, squinting beneath thick grey brows and a brown flat cap older than the century.

“Aye. Name’s Clifton. Folks call me Calder, after the dale. I fix what’s broke. Not miracles, mind. That there’s Jed,” he nodded at a tan spaniel chasing its tail.

Elias stepped around the dog, his gaze brushing over Calder’s jacket, worn thin in places, hands callused from years of labour, and the smoke-and-sheep scent of honest work. “What’s the worst of it?”

Calder straightened with a grunt, his spine cracking like a flagpole.

“Depends what you count. Roof’s gone on the east side of the stables. Fence on the south field’s half-rotted. Pond’s silted. Kitchen garden’s more weeds than crop. Chimney in the blue bedchamber’s temperamental. Windows rattle like the dead are whisperin’. And I’d not trust the bellpull in the library. Last lad what yanked it got hit wi’ a plaster cherub.”

Elias’s shoulders drooped. “…Right.”

Calder shrugged. “Parish calls it character. I call it work.” He drove one last nail home and wiped his hands on a rag. “But it’s good land. Just needs someone who gives a damn.”

He gave a slow nod. “We’ll start with the roof. And the cherub. One crushed footman is enough for now.”

Calder’s mouth wavered—almost a smile.

As Elias turned, he tugged his collar up and cast another glance at the house. Mooredge Hall didn’t test him. It dared him. In London, reputation was currency. Here, it was muck. You could impress the ton with a well-cut coat and a sharp remark. But in Rookhaven? You had to know when to slaughter, when to seed, and how *not* to insult the blacksmith's mother. Elias would learn quickly. Or at least, he'd learn to look like he had. It would take more than coin to bring the Hall and his name back from the brink. It would take alliances. A wife.

He grimaced.

Not just any wife, a quiet one. Decorative. Undemanding. A woman whose reputation gleamed, polished to perfection, and who required nothing true in return. He could hardly fault the plan. It had served his mother well enough. Marriage as transaction. Reputation as a shield.

* * *

The following morning, Elias was on horseback, riding the rutted track from Mooredge toward Rookhaven. The road was narrow, flanked by dry stone walls and hedgerows hacked back into submission. Sheep huddled in the hollows like gossiping widows, unmoved by passing men or weather.

He hadn't intended to ride out. But after Maud tried to serve him herring for breakfast, he'd had enough. And he needed stone, and maybe someone with a hammer that didn't predate the Reformation. He'd heard of a stone-yard up past the church. Likely overpriced. But it was Yorkshire. One took what one could get.

The church came into view: a squat Norman building with ivy climbing the crooked tower like it meant to take the building down with it. Neglect left the graveyard beside it overgrown, and its iron gate hung half open, like a broken invitation.

A voice called out: "Lord Blackstone!"

Elias reined in, his horse tossing its head.

A man approached from the church path, barely thirty-five, black collar crisp, boots muddied, and a genial expression Elias mistrusted.

"Reverend Ward," the man said with a pleasant nod. "I thought I might see you this week. Word travels faster than carts 'round here."

Elias inclined his head. "You have the advantage of me."

"I'm the vicar of Rookhaven parish. Local guide, occasional moral compass, and sometimes broker in souls and storm damage. And most weeks, the latter is trickier."

"I'll keep that in mind."

The Reverend's smile stayed soft, but his eyes were shrewd, a blue that was a touch too cold. "We don't get many new residents. Especially not ones with duelling reputations."

"Of course," Elias said. "First week back in Yorkshire and already the vicar knows which end of a pistol I favour."

"The Lord forgives," Ward replied, voice light. "I merely officiate. And I've conducted funerals for men with worse hobbies."

Elias wasn't sure whether he liked him or wanted to throw him in the silted pond. "I'm bound for the stone-yard," Elias said instead.

"Ah, you'll want Hargreaves, fourth mile past the Ashcroft mill road. Don't let his son handle the order. The boy can't count to twenty without taking off his boots. Avoid Ellis & Wren if you value your coin. They cut with chalk, and half your load will crumble before Michaelmas."

Elias shifted his grip on the reins, leather creaking softly. "And what's the cost of such insight in Rookhaven?"

"First visits are free. After that, you pay in wine or gossip. I take either." There was a flicker—not quite menace, not quite jest. Something *curated*.

Elias studied him. "You're not like most vicars."

"I'm not," Reverend Ward said with a grin never shifting. "Now, you'd best ride on. Looks like we'll have weather by noon."

Elias glanced at the sky. "This *is* weather."

"That," the vicar said, pointing to the shifting grey mass above the hills, "is *Yorkshire* weather."

The horse stamped once. Elias gave a clipped nod. "Reverend."

"Stop by the rectory sometime," the man called after him. "I've got tea. And a roof that only leaks in two places."

Elias clicked his tongue and nudged his horse forward, the muddy road welcoming him back with a familiar squelch.

He wasn't sure what to make of the vicar. Too familiar by half. Too observant, and far too polished in a village full of stone and soot. Maybe that was Yorkshire. Or maybe—it was the most well-mannered trap he'd ever walked into.

4

Chapter Four

The road to the stone-yard veered west, skirting the edge of the Ashcroft estate. The sky sulked, clouds swollen with promised rain. Elias urged his horse into a slow canter. His mood—like the sky—had been greyed out for days. But solitude had its merits: no staring servants or dead-eyed portraits.

The thunder of hooves, fast and unrelenting, echoed off the stone walls of the narrow lane. Elias wheeled his horse around, frowning at the bend behind. No one rode like that unless they were foolish, reckless, or late to their own funeral.

A woman appeared, rounding the corner at a gallop, skirts hitched, dark hair streaming, posture too confident by half. Her grey mare looked well-bred but badly managed, mouth foaming, eyes wild with the thrill of the run. Elias barely had time to react.

She spotted him at the last moment and heaved the reins with a sturdy command. Her horse veered, clipping the edge of Elias's stirrup, both mounts danced, rearing in the churned mud. He steadied his own with a curse under his breath.

She sat hers like a cavalryman. No flinching, or apology, just boots firm in the stirrups and one gloved hand on the reins, the other brushing wind-blown hair from her cheek.

The woman scowled. "You might try keeping to the verge next time. Some of us actually ride."

"You call that riding?"

She smirked. "I call it moving forward at speed. What you were doing looked more like sulking on horseback."

He exhaled through his nose. "Are you—hurt?"

"*Most* men would've doffed their hat or yielded the lane."

"A gentleman removes his hat when invited. As for yielding—" he paused, tightening his grip on the reins, "I've had quite enough of that lately."

"Well," she said crisply, "I'm not in the habit of apologising for riding as I please. This is not London, Lord Blackstone. We're not expected to mince about like prized spaniels."

He blinked. "You know who I am?"

"Of course. Everyone does. You're the scandal, fresh from London."

"And you are?"

She offered a dazzling smile. "Florence Ashcroft. Of Calderbank Mills. You're trespassing on our timber road."

He glanced at the lane. "I thought this was public access."

"It is," she said sweetly. "But we maintain it. So if you're going to sulk in the middle of it, do keep to the edge." She nudged her mare forward, not bothering to wait for a farewell.

Elias watched her disappear into the fogged distance, a blur of self-possession and flying mud. Florence Ashcroft. No manners, and apparently no fear of galloping headlong into a baron. He wasn't sure whether to be offended or enthralled.

There was something about the way she looked straight

through him. She didn't simper. She *challenged.* And what unsettled him most was not that she had bested him, but that part of him liked it.

Elias debated whether to ride straight back to Mooredge, instruct his solicitor to purchase the Ashcroft estate, and build a bloody wall through it. Instead, he turned his horse toward the stone yard.

He found it on the far edge of Rookhaven, behind a rust-streaked red gate and a wall that looked like its own advertisement. Piles of slate, limestone, and reclaimed brick rose in uneven stacks, guarded by a black terrier with one eye and a bark like judgment.

A man emerged from the shed, wiping his hands on his shirt and squinting beneath a now black cap that might once have belonged to a baker or a thief.

"Help you?"

"I need roof tile," Elias said. "Stone flags if you've got them. Black, preferably. And something suitable for the stables."

The man looked him up and down, eyes lingering on the damp boots and coat spattered with Rookhaven's finest filth.

"You're the Blackstone lad, then."

Elias didn't flinch. "Lord Blackstone, yes."

The change was immediate. The man stepped forward, more respectful now, still rough, but tempered with something else, memory, maybe, or past loyalty.

"I'm Hargreave. We cut decent. Don't try Wren & Ellis. They'll weigh your purse heavier than your order."

"I've been warned."

"I knew your father, the Baron," Hargreave said, voice lowering as though out of respect or habit. "Came here once wi' plans for a carriage house. Said he wanted to make the Hall self-sufficient. Talked about mills, tenant farms, hiring local lads. Never got to it, mind."

Elias's jaw tightened. "He died before he could."

"Aye," Hargreave said, thumb worrying the edge of his notebook. "Shame. Had a head full of plans once, he did. Before London swallowed him. Never thought I'd see him trading stone himself, either. But he came here often enough in the early days. Checked the quarry work, argued prices himself. Could tell he cared about the place. About the people."

Elias studied the ground, silent.

Hargreave went on anyway, in that blunt Yorkshire way. "But then came the politics. Summoned down south more months than he were up here. Heard he'd a seat at Quarter Sessions. Talked of enclosing the west pastures and bringing in new sheep blood. Put his name behind militia recruiting—proud as anything when they marched past the market cross. Always running after summat bigger than his own land." The foreman's voice dropped a little. "Aye, he were a busy man. But there's only so many committees and elections and dinners a house can stand you missing before it starts to sag."

That last bit hit deeper than Elias wanted to admit. He cleared his throat and straightened.

"Didn't expect to see you buying yer own stone, lad," Hargreave added, with a trace of admiration now.

"Didn't expect to need so much of it," he said wryly.

"Very good. How many feet?"

Elias gave him the figures. Hargreave listened without interruption and jotted them down.

"Gi' me three days. Might even throw in a discount, seein' as you didn't turn yer nose up at the gate."

"And here I thought Yorkshiremen didn't believe in charity."

"Nobility discount," Hargreave said, deadpan. "Only applies when they look worn out."

Elias almost smiled.

* * *

By the time Elias returned to Mooredge, the light had soured, and the clouds were gathering like creditors. The ride back had done little to improve his mood. The horse was lathered. His coat was stiff with dried mud. And his boots bore a crust of Rookhaven that refused to come clean. Between dodging cart ruts and negotiating roof tiles, he'd begun to suspect Yorkshire itself had doubled its grudge against the Blackstones.

The stable lad barely glanced at him. Either the novelty had worn off, or Elias looked too much like work.

Inside, the hall yawned with silence. The fire in the drawing room had gone out. The sconces hadn't been lit. A draught crept along the floor, and the rug coiled at the corner as if trying to trip him out of spite.

He walked to the library. It was the only room with a lit hearth and a door that stayed shut. The books smelled musty, but they were silent company and didn't ask questions. He tossed his gloves onto the desk and stood by the fire.

Florence Ashcroft, new money, not titled, just entitled. That damned smile. Not a flirt's smile, but the sort of smile one gave a man right before overtaking him on a hill: bright, fleeting, and smugly superior.

He found himself annoyed that she hadn't asked him. Well, *anything*, she seemed to know all she needed to know. It was maddening. It was... *refreshing*. And that was a problem.

The fire crackled. Elias peered into the flames. He didn't like her. He was simply aware of her. And that, he told himself, would pass. He had come north to forget London, rebuild Mooredge, and restore what could be saved. He had not come to be antagonised by a mill owner's daughter with windblown hair and murder in her seat.

5

Chapter Five

The wind prowled the moor like a jealous banshee, and Mooredge's ancient timbers groaned like bones too old to remember comfort. The fire had sputtered overnight, and the mattress—stiff as a church pew—had conspired with the sheets to flay Elias where he lay.

He dressed in silence. No valet, no sleep, just the dull weight of Yorkshire pressing against his skull.

Downstairs, there was coffee, though scorched, and the toast curled like dried parchment. He poured a cup anyway, sipped, and grimaced. His saving grace was that no one attempted conversation. Until Mrs Vale appeared, her tone dry as ever.

"There's someone waiting, my lord."

Elias glanced up with suspicion, a headache tightening behind his eyes. "A tradesman?"

"A boy."

"Tell him to return when his voice breaks."

She didn't so much as flinch. "He says he wishes to apply for the position of valet."

"I didn't advertise for a valet."

"You said you required one."

"I also remarked upon needing a new roof. Shall I accept applicants for that as well?"

Mrs Vale stood straighter. "Might see faster results."

Elias exhaled. "Where is he?"

"This way, sir."

With a long-suffering breath, Elias followed her to the small study off the front hall, the only room that didn't reek of mildew and memory. Inside stood a lanky youth of perhaps eighteen. Pale-haired, freckled, and dressed in what was clearly his Sunday best: sleeves too short, optimism too long. He bowed and nearly toppled a vase.

"Lord Blackstone! Sir. I—I heard from Mrs Vale that you were needing a valet. I'm Tom. Tom Wood. I live over at Muckleby End. My brother's a footman at Ashcroft Manor. I've come to… apply for the post."

Elias gave him a long, unimpressed look. "You've never valeted a day in your life."

"I've read a book on it, sir!"

"*You've* read a book," Elias repeated.

"Yes, sir. Twice, in fact. The Gentleman's Gentleman: A Guide to Civilised Service, *by Mr Peebles."*

"Ah, well. If Mr Peebles is prepared to vouch for you, how can I refuse?"

"I can press trousers… nearly, and boots shine like mirrors when I'm done with 'em. Numbers come easy, sir. I keep the parish books on Sundays. I know this land better than most. All the back ways from Calderbank Mill to the far edge of the Ashcroft estate. There's old smugglers' tracks, half-hidden bridleways, even a dry creek bed you can follow straight under their eastern hedge if you're light on yer feet."

Elias rubbed a hand across his face. "Ashcroft?"

"Ashcroft," Tom said, nodding fast. "Miss Ashcroft runs near everything now. Her father's ill, summat slow. He doesn't take meetings no more, stays at home with his tonic. So it's her name on the orders, her voice the men answer to. Course, not everyone likes it; she's a woman, after all. Some say she'll have to marry, to keep a hold on it."

Elias observed the freckled boy, nervous, possibly delusional, but undeniably keen. And he seemed clever enough to watch and learn, a skill surpassing half the aristocracy.

"Tom," Elias said. "You cannot press trousers. You've never folded a cravat. And I'm fairly sure your idea of decanting brandy involves a bucket and a brief prayer."

Tom straightened his spine. "But I'm a quick study, sir."

"And if you scald my shirts or starch my hair?"

"I'll eat my hat, sir. Whole."

Elias eyed him, weary and resigned. "We'll call it a week's probation. If I'm not bleeding, ablaze, or reduced to shirt sleeves by next Sunday, you stay."

Tom beamed. "Thank you, my lord!"

"And cease calling me 'my lord' every third word."

"Yes, my l—yes. Sir."

"Hell," Elias muttered. He had a valet. Of sorts.

He had to admit the boy knew the village. And the Ashcrofts. And if Elias was to rebuild Mooredge from its broken bones, he'd need more than stone. He'd need eyes, ears, and hands that weren't afraid of ink and mud. And maybe a bit of mad loyalty.

* * *

Calder had appeared during the afternoon, armed with another list of grievances. Nothing dramatic, just the slow, persistent erosion of a house trying to rot around him. By the time Elias returned to the study, late afternoon had given way to dusk, the Hall had sunk into heavy quiet, and the air carried the brittle, bone-deep chill Mooredge wore like a second skin.

Supper had come and gone. Maud had prepared sweetbreads, three kinds of root vegetables, and a sauce that tasted of regret. Elias had forced down enough to be polite and poured himself a brandy to make peace with his stomach.

Tom hovered outside the study doorway, not quite sure if he should announce himself or vanish into the fading wallpaper.

Elias didn't look up. He gave a dismissive flick of the wrist. "Sit. Briefly. Don't make a habit of it."

Tom perched on the edge of a chair like it might ignite beneath him.

Elias took a sip of brandy. "Tell me about the Ashcrofts. Everything you know."

Tom blinked. "The Ashcrofts, sir?"

"Is your hearing poor, or just your wits?"

"No, sir! I—wasn't sure where to start." He rubbed his palms on his trousers. "Well. Mr Ashcroft, he's been unwell for a while now, and when he does show his face, it's usually to sign something Miss Florence's already arranged."

Elias squinted into the fire like it owed him money. "Yes, and the daughter?"

"Miss Ashcroft?" Tom's voice brightened. "She's the one people talk about. Took over near everything at the mill. Changed the lighting. Brought in engineers from Leeds last winter to fit new machinery. She *warned* the overseers that they would be replaced if they touched the weavers.

Elias's brow rose a fraction. "Progressive."

"Some say so. Others think she's reckless." Tom lowered his voice conspiratorially. "But it's running better than ever. More orders. Fewer injuries. Even the lads who grumbled have stopped. And there's talk of her designing new looms herself, as if *she* were an engineer!"

"Outrageous," he said, shaking his head.

"She's not married, sir."

Elias blinked. "That wasn't remotely part of the question."

"Just saying, sir."

Silence stretched. Elias swirled the brandy in his glass and looked at Tom sideways. "What else?"

"She's got hot water in the Manor's kitchen, gas lighting in three rooms. Even a piano from London! The servants say she reads newspapers from France. Rumour is she wrote a letter to the mayor in Manchester and he actually replied."

Elias huffed a quiet laugh. "A woman with opinions—how terrifying."

"She's clever," Tom said, "—for a woman, I mean. That's what my brother says."

"You've said enough." Elias stood.

Tom shot up as well, hands behind his back, trying not to grin.

"Have a bath brought up," Elias said. "Hot, if possible. And see if we have any towels that the local wildlife hasn't chewed.

It was a disaster. The water was hauled from the scullery pump and heated in a dented copper kettle. It was lukewarm by the time it reached the tin tub in his chamber. The towels smelled musty and bore holes that suggested generations of moths had hosted feasts upon them.

Elias dried himself and went sprawling when the frayed rug

beneath his feet recoiled like a trap.

The bed. God above. The sheets, allegedly replaced, had all the softness of sackcloth. Linen, perhaps, but now so worn and starched, they rasped against his skin like dry leaves. He lay on his back, staring at the cracked plaster overhead. His head ached. His spine ached, and his *dignity* ached.

"This place," he muttered into the gloom, "is a personal vendetta from my father." He rolled to one side and winced. Miss Florence Ashcroft had gas-lighting. And a piano. And soft towels—probably. He didn't need a piano. Or newspapers from France. He needed sheets. The county bled linen and worsted. How hard could it be?

6

Chapter Six

The Ashcroft Mill sat low in Calderbank valley like a beast, crouched and waiting, the rhythmic churn of gears and pulleys, the hiss of steam, and the distant thump of the looms.

He dismounted near the front office, handed the reins to a lad who gawked at his coat like it was a museum exhibit. He stepped through the doors with every intention of making this visit brief, efficient, and *beneath* his dignity.

He'd braced himself for the noise of the mill, but hadn't braced nearly enough for the heat and the scent of oil, wool, and metal.

"Lord Blackstone." Florence Ashcroft's unimpressed voice cut through the clatter like a whip. She stood at the foot of the stairwell, still as judgement blocking the step not with defiance, but with authority. A ledger balanced in one hand, hair pinned almost properly—though the ink smudge on her wrist, and the blaze in her eyes, spoke of a woman accustomed to work, not pretence.

"Miss Ashcroft," Elias returned, his tone dry enough to parch stone. "Twice now, you've appeared where I least expect you. I'm beginning to suspect it's deliberate."

She didn't smile. "You think highly of yourself if you believe I schedule my day around alarming *you*."

Heat pricked beneath his collar, his fingers drummed once against his thigh before he stilled them. "You manage a mill, command a horse, and still find time to chastise the idle. Tell me, Miss Ashcroft—" He frowned. "Is there anything you leave to mere mortals?"

For the briefest second, her grip tightened on the ledger's edge, long enough to betray that she'd heard his question as he'd meant it.

She straightened and met his gaze head-on. "Fainting—or fluttering," she said evenly. "I've little time for theatrics, Lord Blackstone." The smallest curve of her mouth followed. She looked away first, not because she had to, but more like she chose to let him stew in it.

He opened his mouth and closed it again. Words were waiting, but none he dared give her. Florence's lips curved into something maddeningly close to a smirk. "That's what I thought," she said, turning on her heel, leaving the scent of ink and cotton in her wake.

Elias exhaled, his eyes following her despite himself. "I came," he called after her, "about linen. And cotton. Bedding, specifically."

She glanced over her shoulder, and he added, with less certainty, the words catching in his throat: "I… find myself in need."

"So the mighty Lord Blackstone seeks salvation by way of *sheets*?"

Elias's shoulders stiffened. "They're more scourge than

comfort."

Florence tilted her head and swept him with her gaze like a catalogue entry she wasn't impressed by. "A tragic tale indeed. And here I thought Yorkshire was known for hardier men."

He scowled. "I came for trade, not mock*ery.*"

"We offer both," she shot back, "generously."

He held her stare. Somewhere between laughing and throttling her, he realised he'd quite lost track of which he preferred.

"We've bolt cloth and linen blends in the back," she said over her shoulder, already moving, ledger tucked neatly under one arm. "I'll show you, provided you don't faint at the sight of a spinning Jenny."

He followed, his spine rigid, hands clasped behind his back to keep them still. The air between them was charged, though whether it was vexation or something altogether more dangerous, he couldn't yet say. "You're not like the other ladies in town."

She glanced back, voice dry as chalk. "Praise be."

His mouth tightened. "I meant—"

"I know precisely what you meant."

Elias narrowed his eyes, pacing a step behind her. "You don't trouble yourself much with decorum, do you?"

She glanced back, mouth twitching. "I do. I just don't waste it."

His brow furrowed. "On me?"

Her navy skirts skimmed the floorboards as she turned into a narrow storeroom. Bolts of fabric lined the walls. Cotton dust hung in the air, and light filtered dimly through high windows.

Elias lingered at the threshold. It was no ordinary room, more like her dominion—and it seemed he had no business standing there.

She stopped at the worktable and fixed him with a cool gaze. "I keep my manners where they're useful, Lord Blackstone. They don't stretch to men who barge in barking about bedding, as if they've mistaken me for their draper on Bond Street."

She reached for a bolt, slid it free from the stack, and spread it across the worktable with a practised snap. She patted her hand against the fabric.

"This won't flay you alive," she said. "Soft weave. For skin no longer accustomed to *Yorkshire weather.*" Her eyes flicked up long enough to make the implication sting.

Elias stayed where he was, palms opening and closing at his sides, willing himself not to rise to the bait. He stepped closer, closing the last of the space between them. His hand skimmed over the fabric, testing it, weighing it. It was finer than anything Mooredge deserved. Finer than *he* deserved, if he was honest.

"It'll do," he said, his voice low, almost grudging.

Florence glanced up, and her expression shifted. Not softness—not that, but a flicker of something, perhaps appraisal. Maybe even curiosity. Whatever it was, it passed and smoothed back into something neutral. "You're *not* what I expected," she murmured.

He tilted his head, catching the faintest edge of her gaze before she could drop it. His mouth curved.

"And what, Miss Ashcroft, did you expect?"

"A Lord," she said coolly. "All silks, sighs, and gentlemen's clubs. With no notion of what a leaking roof means for the servant sleeping under it."

Elias met her scrutiny squarely, eyes flaring. "My roof nearly killed me on Tuesday. And I've spent more hours in a stone yard this week than I ever did at White's."

Her eyes gleamed at that, like she'd been hoping for this admission. "So you're not entirely ornamental after all."

He snorted. "I sign ledgers. Occasionally, issue commands no one listens to—Calder runs the place. I walk the grounds looking purposeful and hope no one asks me what a barley drill is." His tone was smooth, the words landed like a jest, but the edge was there if you knew where to look. "But thank you," he added dryly, "for the promotion. Ornamental is a step up from cautionary tale." He hadn't meant to say quite so much. But something about her made honesty feel less like a weakness and more like a provocation.

"You," he murmured, voice low and tight, "are infuriating."

"Good," she murmured, the curve of her mouth belying her words. "We'll get along splendidly."

She turned toward the shelves, fingers trailing along the edge of a linen bolt. Her eyes flashed, a gauntlet thrown.

"There are any number of parish gatherings," she continued. "Dancing. Parading of livestock. The harvest festival. You will be expected to attend, of course. I do hope you endure them better than you endure your scratchy sheets."

He huffed something between a laugh and a protest, though he'd never admit to either. "Heaven forbid—I came to Yorkshire to escape society, not to be paraded through it again."

She glanced sceptically at him over her shoulder. "And yet here you are. Buying cloth and making conversation."

A smile threatened at the edge of his mouth but never fully formed. "This, " he drawled, waving his palm, "is hardly society."

She moved past him with unhurried authority, brushing cotton from her sleeve as though he were merely another speck of dust.

"No," she said, almost to herself. "This isn't society, Lord Blackstone. This is Calderbank."

The words caught him off guard, less an insult, more a declaration. *Calderbank.* Her world. Built from cloth, noise, and competence. Not salons and scandal.

He was still trying to formulate a clever response when she paused at the doorway, glancing back with a knowing smile that didn't reach her eyes.

"I'll send the order this afternoon. Try not to be scandalised by the weaver—she's far hardier than you."

Before he could reply, a young millworker appeared at her shoulder, cap in hand, worry on his brow.

"Miss Ashcroft," he said. "It's the loom again. It's smoking."

Florence was gone before Elias could speak, her voice already ringing down the corridor like a bell. He watched her go—struck not by her beauty, but by her command. The mill was hers, and Elias knew better than to challenge a woman obeyed by a hundred men.

Besides, he was still trying to understand what a culvert was.

7

Chapter Seven

Dinner was tepid soup and tougher beef, and Elias couldn't decide which irked him more, the meat's resistance or the company.

Lady Cheverley regarded him as though boredom itself might claim her as its next victim.

She announced airily, as though discussing the weather, "We've been invited to the Harvest Ball."

Elias didn't bother looking up from his plate. "Decline."

She tilted her head, her dark eyes flashing a little brighter than the candlelight. "I already accepted."

He set his knife down with a faint clatter. His jaw was tight enough to ache. "Mother."

She frowned at him. "Elias."

"I've no interest in being paraded before a flock of half-bankrupt baronets and desperate debutantes," Elias said, his tone dry enough to splinter. "Half the room wouldn't shake my hand publicly, old friends of Father's included."

Lady Cheverley swirled her wine. "That's the old blood for you. Sanctimonious as priests and just as prone to sin behind closed doors."

He scoffed. "They forget their own sons have done worse."

"They forget because they can afford to. You, my darling, are new scandal in old stone. They haven't decided yet if you're worth forgiving."

Elias's mouth twisted. "And you think this ball will convince them?"

"I think," she said sweetly, "that new money doesn't ask nearly so many questions. And their daughters are hungrier."

The words dropped between them like a stone in water. The only sound that followed was the faint scrape of her knife against porcelain as she returned to her plate, perfectly composed. Lady Cheverley reached for her napkin and dabbed her mouth with the serenity of someone who'd already won.

"Besides," she continued, "it's at Wrenthorpe Manor. Lovely house. Terrible roof. Old money with no actual money. They say the daughter is quite accomplished at watercolours.

Elias pinched the bridge of his nose. "God help me."

She smiled, folding her napkin with precision. "You'll dance, you'll smile, and you'll charm whoever needs charming. Especially Mrs Fairfax, she'll be watching."

He dropped his hand. "Fairfax?"

"She's on every committee that matters and three that don't. People trust her opinion, foolish, but true. If she sees you leave early, the entire village will know by morning."

She dabbed at her lips. "She collects gossip like some women collect teacups."

He muttered, "I would rather leap from the terrace."

Her eyes sparkled as she rose, her smile pointed as a blade. "Well, make sure you're wearing something worth dying in."

* * *

The harvest moon hung low and heavy over Calderbank, casting the moors in silver shadow. The weeks had passed in a blur of grudging repairs, and now, almost before he'd realised it, the Ball had arrived.

At Mooredge, candles flared against darkened windows, and the faint chill of autumn seeped through every crack. Elias stood at the threshold of his chamber, already regretting the evening ahead.

Tom was waiting with a pile of linen and unearned optimism. "Evening, sir. I've been consulting Peebles' Guide to Ball Preparations," the lad announced proudly, balancing what looked like enough starch to stop a cavalry charge.

Elias narrowed his brow as he shut the door. "Ah, yes, Peebles. Isn't he the sadist who believes discomfort is the hallmark of breeding?"

Tom beamed as if that were a compliment. "I think you'll be pleased."

He was not. The coat, while passable, was deep navy with frayed cuffs, salvageable with a good press. Miraculously, the breeches matched. The boots gleamed to a blinding shine, which suggested Tom had nearly lost a thumb in the effort. But the cravat. The cravat was pink.

Elias approached it as though it might leap for his throat. "What in God's name is this?"

Tom glanced at the offending scrap of silk, unruffled. "Cravat, sir."

"Yes—why is it the colour of a blushing piglet?"

Tom winced, but held his ground. "Laundry mix-up, sir.

One of the maids washed it wi' a red thing. Curtain, maybe. Tablecloth. Hard to say."

Elias glowered at it like it had personally insulted him. "It's... pink."

Tom cleared his throat. "Soft rose."

Elias's lip curled. "It's vengeance in cotton form."

Tom hesitated, then brightened. "I can try bleaching it—"

Elias waved him off. "No. At this point—it's a warning."

Tom lifted it earnestly. "You'll wear it?"

Elias squinted at the offending fabric and exhaled through his nose. The thing practically glowed against the navy of his coat, obscene in its softness. "I'll wear it," he said at last, voice flat as stone. "And when someone asks, I'll claim it's been dyed in the blood of my enemies."

He glanced at his reflection holding the cravat at his throat, and added under his breath: "If nothing else, it should keep the debutantes at bay."

Tom, hearing none of the muttered cursing, beamed and straightened the knot with reverence. "Very good, sir. Very good indeed."

Downstairs, Lady Cheverley was already dressed in midnight-grey silk, her diamonds catching the candlelight, like tiny knives at her throat. Elias strongly suspected they'd been purchased with husband number two's investments and husband number one's regrets.

She looked up at the sound of his boots, took in the sight of him, and pressed a gloved hand delicately to her lips.

"That's bold, darling," she murmured, eyes flicking to the pink at his throat.

Elias descended the last step with all the dignity he could summon. "Say nothing."

She beamed. "I've always liked you in colour."

He gave her a flat look. "It's not colour—It's a textile tragedy."

She peered at him once more, head to toe, before she offered a low, amused hum, as though she were already imagining how to turn his misery into her amusement

She tucked her hand into his arm as the carriage arrived. "Smile, my darling. It might confuse the locals."

* * *

Wrenthorpe Manor had once been the pride of the county. It had not yet accepted the change.

The chandeliers shone valiantly, though half the crystals bore the dull film of neglect. The gold cornicing peeled at the edges like old wallpaper. And the floral arrangements—towering, fragrant, and wilting—reeked of desperation. Someone had paid handsomely for appearances, and not a farthing for subtlety.

Elias adjusted the fit of his coat as he stepped into the main hall, the press of bodies and candlelight immediately oppressive. His eyes swept the crowd instinctively, already cataloguing the room. He wasn't sure what he was looking for, perhaps an escape or a decent bottle of wine.

His mother swept ahead, all elegance and calculation, pausing to greet their hostess at the foot of the grand staircase. Lady Wrenthorpe—thin-lipped, lacquered, and watchful—looked Elias over like a butcher appraising a particularly troublesome side of beef.

"Lady Cheverley. Lord Blackstone," she said, voice polished to a hard shine. "Delighted you could join us."

There was the slightest stress on *could,* as though their attendance were a regrettable necessity rather than a triumph.

Elias inclined his head, his expression schooled into polite indifference. "Thank you for the invitation."

Lady Wrenthorpe's smile twitched. "We do so value tradition. And your family, of course, has long roots in the county." The implication hung in the air like damp lace: roots didn't always mean flowers. "And we must keep society lively in the north. Even if it means importing eligible bachelors from London. You'll find no shortage of company tonight." She leaned in ever so slightly, her eyes flicking toward the crush of young women near the dance floor. "I believe the ratio of unmarried ladies to titled men this evening is highly favourable."

Elias caught the faint scent of violets and determination and managed not to flinch. Terrifying, he thought. Absolutely terrifying.

Lady Wrenthorpe's eyes glittered as she pivoted and gestured to a girl standing behind her, perhaps twenty-one, wide-eyed, her cheeks too pink, and her posture so rigid it seemed she might crack if she bent at all.

"My daughter, Honoria," Lady Wrenthorpe announced, her tone both possessive and expectant.

Honoria Wrenthorpe stepped forward as though walking into an ambush, curtsying low, her face hovered up to meet his, then darted away. "It's lovely to meet you, my lord," she mumbled.

Elias inclined his head, offering what he hoped passed for a reassuring smile. "The pleasure is mine, Miss Wrenthorpe."

Behind Honoria, Lady Wrenthorpe's demeanour subtly changed; her mouth tightened, and a frigid light sparked behind her eyes. The message was clear: Try harder. Smile more. Be more. Marry *him*. Honoria seemed to feel it too. Her shoulders stiffened as her hands knotted in her pale skirts.

Elias held her gaze for a moment longer, noting the quiet panic there, and thought with grim certainty that this was not the chit he would marry to repair his reputation. He only hoped his mother understood that before she did something spectacularly inconvenient.

Elias inclined his head, murmured something about refreshing his drink—a lie so polite it barely registered as one, and slipped away before Lady Wrenthorpe could fasten the last of the matrimonial ropes around his neck.

8

Chapter Eight

The ballroom was already thick with heat and candlelight, the crush almost suffocating. He lingered at the edges, observing the crowd with the cool disinterest of a man appraising livestock.

There were men of every stripe here: one fellow who had made his fortune in tea and wouldn't stop *steeping* everyone in the story; another in a silk waistcoat so vulgar it should have been banned from polite company, and a few who thought shouting their fortunes across the room might convince someone—perhaps even themselves—they'd earned them honestly.

Elias endured them all with the kind of chilly, well-practised indifference that old money could pull off, a faint nod here, a thin smile there, all while mentally mapping the nearest exits and weighing how long civility would require him to remain.

At the far side of the ballroom, Florence Ashcroft was laughing beside Honoria Wrenthorpe, the two of them standing together like a study in contrast: one pale and delicate, the other alive with confidence and fire. Florence wore a gown of deep forest green, simple in cut, with no frills or lace to soften it. The effect was clean, striking, and undeniable. And she was not wearing gloves. *Wicked*, and somehow intentional.

He watched her longer than he should have. And she noticed. She looked up without flinching, head tilted ever so slightly—*Still staring?* her expression seemed to say. *I must look unfamiliar in silk and candlelight.*

Then she looked away, a ghost of a smile playing at her mouth. A silent triumph, beneath her notice to claim.

Elias turned, plucking a glass of wine with enough force to startle the footman. His irritation directed at himself, at her, and at this northern circus masquerading as society. He took a sip and let his gaze roam—anywhere but the corner where she still stood, burning brighter than the damned chandeliers.

He couldn't avoid staring forever. Better to let the crowd swallow him, dull the flash of her smile with meaningless talk and terrible wine.

He tried conversation. Endured it. Three dull exchanges, two sharp glances that slid off his collar like raindrops, and one gentleman who said, without irony, "And do you find our Yorkshire air less *charged* than the duelling grounds of Mayfair?"

Elias's smile thinned. "I find the air here cleaner. If one ignores the stench of hypocrisy."

The man blinked. Laughed, too late, then moved on.

Nearby, a silk-clad matron whispered behind a fan. Elias caught only the words "pistol," "mother," and "reckless." He drained half his glass.

Each encounter sharpened the edges of his temper and made the rest of the room look duller, as though someone had painted over it in beige.

He needed air. Or violence. Instead, he found the Reverend.

"Lord Blackstone," came the smooth, amused voice of Reverend Ward, materialising at his elbow like fog. "We meet again."

Elias inclined his head, masking the temper curling in his gut. "Reverend. You're far from your pulpit."

Ward smiled. "I go where the sinners gather."

Elias blinked at him a fraction too long before glancing toward the terrace, where a faint breath of cool air stirred the curtains. A flicker of green skirts, Florence vanished into the night before he could stop himself noticing.

When his eyes returned to Ward, the reverend was already watching him, fixed and uncomfortably still. He sipped his wine as though nothing at all had passed between them.

"You're adjusting to Mooredge, I trust?"

"I'm surviving it," Elias replied, more curtly than he intended.

"Hmm." Ward took another slow sip. "You've drawn interest tonight. But not all eyes here forget so easily."

Elias stilled. "They forget when it suits them."

"Do they?" Ward's voice dipped lower. "Duels leave scars, Lord Blackstone. Not always on the body."

Elias's gaze sharpened.

Ward shrugged casually. "If the apothecary's wife likes you, you're halfway to sainthood round here. Still, some circles forgive faster than others. Provided you give them something else to whisper about."

"Such as?"

Ward's gleaming smile returned. "A wife, perhaps. Something useful to do that doesn't involve pistols."

Elias huffed, his lips twisting into something sour. "Is this where you tell me a wife would do wonders for my reputation?"

Ward swirled the wine in his glass, unfazed. "It would certainly keep tongues busy with more respectable stories. And you'd do better with a steady presence at your side than the reputation you dragged out of London."

Elias's head tilted, eyes narrowing. "Bold advice from a bachelor clergyman. I don't see a Mrs Ward standing at your side. Or is she hiding somewhere in the nave?"

Ward's expression didn't waver, but his mouth curved into something dangerous. "Ah," he said softly. "Yes. Well. Do as I say, not as I do." Ward's tone softened a fraction. "Don't mistake endurance for a plan, Lord Blackstone. It's not."

Elias studied him, unsettled but unwilling to show it. "I'll keep that in mind," he muttered, though he wasn't sure he meant it.

Ward merged back into the crush like smoke through a keyhole. Elias was already moving before he knew why. The air outside bit instantly, the autumn chill curling through his coat and catching in his throat. Above, the sky hung like bruised navy velvet, stars blinking through restless clouds.

He rounded the corner, and there she was. Florence Ashcroft stood backed against the cold stone balustrade, her arms braced, palms out, holding off the swaying bulk of a drunken, vaguely familiar local gentleman. His cravat hung loose, his words thick with wine.

"You're so lovely," he slurred, leaning closer—with the clumsy determination of the truly drunk. "I'd treat you right, Miss Ashcroft. Warm bed… warm hands…"

Florence rose to her full height, her voice iron-wrapped in velvet. "Step back."

"Oh come now, don't be cruel—"

When he reached for her sleeve, Elias didn't think—he

moved.

"Step. Away. From her." His voice cracked like a whip.

The drunk blinked, confused. "Who—is you?"

Elias smiled, but there was no warmth in it. "Her brother," he lied smoothly, stepping closer. "And the next man you'll apologise to if you value your nose."

The man swayed, his eyes darting between them, then he muttered something indistinct and staggered back toward the ballroom, weaving like a ship with one tattered sail.

Florence exhaled but didn't move. Elias turned to her, his gaze raking over her as if checking for damage. "Are you all right?"

Her chin lifted. "Perfectly."

His brows drew tight. "You were backed into a corner—"

"I managed the situation," she cut in, low and precise.

He stepped closer, his voice rising. "By doing what? scolding him until he emptied his stomach on your boots?"

Her eyes flashed. "Would you rather I fainted and let you carry me heroically into the night?"

"I'd prefer if men didn't feel entitled to corner you at all!"

She moved closer, close enough that he could feel her breath. "And I'd prefer if men didn't feel entitled to rescue me without asking."

"I saw a woman in distress—"

"You saw a woman you *decided* was in distress," she snapped.

He leaned in, voice rough. Barely leashed. "You were two seconds away from being mauled." The air between them crackled. The tension in his jaw intensified.

"And you think I haven't faced worse?" she said at last, steady and cold. "This is Yorkshire, my lord. I ride through industrial villages alone. I speak in boardrooms, and I own half the valley.

Do you truly believe I can't handle one snivelling inebriate?"

"Why do you do this?" he demanded.

Her eyes were fixed, cold and gleaming. "Do what?"

"Provoke. Every chance you get."

She didn't move at first, just looked at him like she was measuring a man who'd already come up short. Then stepped closer still. He could feel the chill radiating off her even through the heat of his temper.

Her voice, when it came, was quiet, but it cut like glass: "Because the moment I let a man close enough to help, he'll think he has the right to command."

She let it hang there long enough to burn. Then turned, skirts flaring, boots clicking against stone, and left him standing in the aftermath of something he couldn't take back.

9

Chapter Nine

Florence found Honoria tucked into an alcove beyond the ballroom, half-hidden behind a carved screen, fanning herself with all the bored elegance of a woman trained to endure society without ever enjoying it.

"There you are, Florence said tightly, snatching a goblet from a passing footman, and draining half before Honoria even looked up.

Honoria tilted her head lazily. "Well, good evening to you, too."

Florence hissed through her teeth, the taste of wine doing nothing to blunt the heat in her chest. "Lord Blackstone."

"Ah." Honoria's lips fluttered, as though suppressing a laugh. "That explains the thunderclouds clinging to you. Positively biblical."

Florence dropped into the chair beside her, skirts swishing like an accusation. "He boxed me in on the terrace. After—after I'd already sent some drunken fool on his way. He charged in like I was seconds from fainting. Like I needed saving."

Honoria lowered her fan and glanced at her, blue eyes

dancing. "I do hope you made it clear his gallantry was wasted?"

Florence's mouth tightened into a thin line. "Oh, he got the idea. But he looked at me like…" she stopped, fingers gripping the stem of her glass, "like he pitied me, as though the entire scene was his to command. And I—" she broke off, breath spiking.

Honoria's fan fluttered while peering at the ballroom. "Well," she said at last, voice mild but with an edge to it, "that's what happens when you're the only woman in the room who doesn't swoon at the sight of a title. You confuse them. And confused men," she added with a delicate shrug, "are invariably irritable." Her mouth curved into a smile, eyes sliding to Florence. "He is rather dashing, though. If a little… *murderous*. He terrifies me if I'm honest."

Florence's head snapped up, her reply quick. "He doesn't terrify me."

"Oh?" Honoria's smile turned feline. "Your ears turned pink when you said his name."

"They did not."

"They did. Like a startled rabbit."

Florence scowled into her glass and took another sip, glaring out at the ballroom as though daring it to offend her further.

"He thinks I need protecting. That I ought to be grateful he came charging in like the Duke of Wellington—men like him never believe a woman can save herself."

Honoria hummed. "And yet, you're still talking about him…"

Florence's eyes cut to her like a blade.

Honoria leaned in, lowering her voice to a conspiratorial murmur. "You do know what they say about him in London?"

Florence arched a brow. "I don't deal in gossip."

"That's because you're sensible. I, however, am not." Honoria tapped her fan against her lips.

"There was a duel. Over a woman, they say. Or a debt. Or possibly a scandalous poem."

Florence blinked. "A poem?"

"Well, there was definitely blood. Possibly a dead man. No one quite agrees. Some say he fled to the north to avoid prosecution. Others that he paid to hush it all up."

"And you believe *any* of that?"

"I believe scandal clings to him like perfume. You don't have to believe it, you only have to wonder why no one denies it outright."

Florence's gaze drifted to where Elias stood like a shadow too large for the room, watching everything and nothing all at once.

"Some men walk into a room like they own it," Honoria murmured. "Lord Blackstone walks in like he's already bored of setting it on fire."

Florence rolled the rim of the goblet against her lower lip. "He's not that interesting."

Honoria's fan twitched. "No. Not at all." The music swelled, a waltz, bright and relentless. Honoria groaned. "Mama's going to have me strangled if I don't get up and dance," she muttered. "Half the reason for the ball is to parade me around like a prized lamb." She gave a theatrical shudder. "She's turned down every man who's shown interest so far. Too poor, bookish, or fond of poetry. Heaven forbid I marry someone who likes me."

Florence straightened, a spark of mischief lighting her eyes. "So she's sorting through suitors, then? To find someone *passable*?"

Honoria sighed, her fan drooping. "Precisely. Someone wealthy, titled, and too stupid to notice he's being hunted."

Florence's mouth snapped into something thoughtful. "Hmm. That's rather interesting."

Honoria glanced at her suspiciously. "*Why?*"

"Because," Florence said, swirling her wine, "perhaps I could do the same. Only in reverse order."

Honoria blinked at her. "I beg your pardon?"

Florence leaned in, lowering her voice until the music and laughter outside the screen became a faint thrum. "I don't want an actual marriage," she said, the words tasting strange in her mouth, but truer for being spoken aloud. "I don't want children. I want to run my mills and expand production. Bring in the new looms. Build proper cottages for the workers and their families. I want—" she faltered, "—freedom."

She drew a steady breath, but it caught halfway. "If my father dies—" Her thumb traced the rim of her glass, hard enough to leave a mark. "And he will," she blurted, as if speed might keep the words from settling in her chest "Though he refuses to admit it outright, the doctor said consumption months ago. Slow, but inevitable. And he… he told me last week he wanted to see me married before… before the end. He thinks it will keep me safe. That a husband will take care of me. He doesn't see that it's the very thing I dread most."

Honoria tilted her head, something curious flickering in her eyes.

Florence's voice hardened. "If he dies before I find some way to protect what I've built, the first man to make his claim will force me into wedlock. And some idiot, some soft-palmed heir who's never seen a spindle, will take everything. Everything my father and I worked for."

Her breath shuddered, glaring into the distance as if daring fate to contradict her. "I've seen what marriage and children do to women. It's not safety. It's a cage. So perhaps..."

Honoria gave her a quizzical look.

"Perhaps," Florence said more evenly, "your mother isn't entirely wrong. I could find someone suitable. A shield. A husband in name only who will leave me and my mills well enough alone. If I wait, they'll choose for me. But if I choose wisely, first, then at least the noose is mine to wear,"

Honoria's fan stilled mid-sweep. "And your plan is...?"

Florence grinned, sharp as scissors, and twice as dangerous. "I *deliberately* choose someone who doesn't care a fig for romance. Someone willing to sign his name in the register and disappear to his hunting lodge, leaving me to my work. He gets a quiet, comfortable life. I get my freedom. Everyone wins."

Honoria gasped, though her eyes glittered with barely concealed delight. "Florence Ashcroft," she breathed, "that is sinful."

She took another measured sip, as if congratulating herself on the plan. "No," she corrected, "it's perfect. I'll test them. Strip away the ones who want babies and docile wives. I'll find the one who needs me as much as I *don't* need him."

Honoria's fan resumed its lazy flutter, her voice sly. "And Lord Blackstone?"

Florence's smile turned cold. "Was *never* in the running."

Honoria didn't reply, but the look she gave Florence said, *we'll see about that*.

Florence rose to her full height, chin high, and declared, "We start now!" before sweeping into the ballroom with the poise of a general striding onto the battlefield. Honoria followed, muttering like a weary governess drawn into mischief; she lacked both the power to prevent and the will to resist.

CHAPTER NINE

"You cannot possibly be serious," Honoria hissed as they rejoined the crowd.

Florence didn't so much as glance at her. Her eyes were already sweeping the room, keen and calculating. The crowd swelled beneath the chandeliers, ripe with eligible bachelors, all handpicked by Lady Wrenthorpe's iron-fisted matchmaking. A curated crop of titled or moneyed men, standing like cattle at auction: polished boots, crisp cravats, and varying degrees of disinterest or desperation glinting in their eyes.

Well. Florence thought they'd do nicely. Bar the Reverend, of course, though the idea of including him purely to scandalise the entire process crossed her mind with a satisfying little incline of her lip. She snatched up her dance card and the tiny pencil tied to it with ribbon. The ballroom stretched before her, full of possibilities and pitfalls alike.

"So," she said, pencil poised over the card, "who do you like for candidate number one?"

Honoria's mouth fell open, and she sputtered. "Candidate—Florence, you're treating this like a cattle market!"

Florence gave her a wolfish grin. "Oh, it *is* a cattle market. But I'm the only one honest enough to say so."

Honoria groaned under her breath, fanning herself like a woman condemned.

Florence swept the ballroom with precision, her head tilting to her left. "Tall one, by the refreshment table," she murmured, her voice brisk.

Honoria followed her line of sight and sighed. "Lord Marchwood. Old money. Hunting estate near York. Possibly the slowest conversationalist I've ever endured, I once watched him try to form a sentence and nearly died of old age before he finished it."

Florence grinned. She jotted a crisp little *M* on her dance card.

"Blond one. Green waistcoat. By the musicians."

Honoria snorted. "Mr Fenwick. Son of a shipping magnate. Laughs like a drainpipe being strangled, but wealthy, tolerably polite, and, to my knowledge, disease-free."

"F," Florence said, scribbling neatly. "Dark one, near the pillar?" she added after a pause, her voice all business and concentration.

Honoria leaned over far enough to glimpse him and wrinkled her nose. "Sir Ransom. Inherited his title from a great-uncle who bred bulldogs. Unremarkable but well-behaved. No ill-doing that I've heard, unless you count his appalling dancing."

"R," Florence noted, amused.

Honoria's gaze flicked toward the far corner. "There's Mr Layton, of course. You always admired his ideas—all that reform talk and his obsession with clean water."

Florence hesitated, pencil hovering mid-air. "Yes, well. He seems earnest."

"That's practically a love confession from you," Honoria said, eyes alight with the smug satisfaction of being right.

And so it continued, Florence the shrewd-eyed hawk, and Honoria the weary, muttering commentator at her side.

Each man was studied, dismissed or noted: those who danced with grace, those who spoke kindly to the footmen, those who neither leered nor droned on about their investments. By the time she finished, Florence's dance card looked less like a list of partners and more like a battlefield map, each name marked like a strategic position.

"Ten," she declared at last, triumphant, pencil held like a sword. "That's the list."

"And what, pray, are you planning to *do* with them?"

Florence's smile was wicked enough to curdle cream. "I'll host them all to supper at Ashcroft Manor, two weeks hence."

Honoria nearly dropped her fan. "A private supper. With ten men—*alone*?"

"Of course not alone, don't be absurd, the invitations will bear my father's name, but the guest list will be entirely mine. And you'll be there—half the house staff will be there. But I'll host it. And then..." she tapped the card against her chin, eyes glinting, "I'll choose the one who proves the least objectionable."

"Florence Ashcroft, you're treating this like a military campaign."

Florence didn't even flinch. "It is. And I intend to win."

Honoria leaned closer, lowering her voice. "And what if... what if one of them actually falls in love with you?"

Florence's pencil stilled. "He'll be disqualified," she said, as she strode into the crowd, head high, skirts sweeping behind her like a battle standard. And Florence, despite herself, caught the flicker of Lord Blackstone's gaze, dark and far too focused.

10

Chapter Ten

By Thursday, Mooredge was crawling with tradesmen. The gardens rang with the thud of hammers and the clatter of scaffolding, punctuated by the occasional bark of a foreman and the metallic scrape of nails being prised from old timbers.

Elias stood outside the stables, arms folded, watching two bricklayers argue over whether the entire roof needed replacing or just the worst half.

From the smell alone, he was inclined to say: tear it down, salt the earth, and be done with it. He didn't know the first thing about roofing, but Calder had warned him to stop nodding like a London solicitor and start asking questions like a man who lived with his decisions. So he did. He asked, listened, and scribbled notes in the margin of an estate ledger he didn't fully understand and pretended he did.

And yet something curious was happening. There were bones beneath the dust and damp. Good ones. Stones that still held warmth if you pressed a hand to them. He'd thought the whole place was unsalvageable, but now, with each rotten beam removed and every slate replaced, something stirred.

By the time he'd sketched out further plans with the carpenter and instructed the tiler on replacing the leaky scullery roof, a strange and insistent thing began to creep in. Vision. Not mastery. Not pride. But that sharp, quiet thing his father used to chase between the ledgers and land deeds, the belief that a place could be more than its walls. He could see it now, not just repaired but restored.

Restoring the house was one thing. Fending off whatever theatre his mother was plotting was another. Lady Cheverley, his dear mother, swept into the morning room in *purple*.

Elias froze. His mother, widow of two titled men and self-appointed queen of London's quieter scandals, had worn black for over a year. Grey for five weeks. And now here she stood, statuesque and unapologetic in a perfectly tailored mauve walking dress, her bonnet trimmed with plum ribbon and a small cluster of lavender pinned at her shoulder.

"And here I thought this house had seen all the ghosts it could bear," he asked.

Lady Cheverley's eyes narrowed, flint-bright. "Well, you'd best make room, darling. This ghost has no intention of fading quietly."

"That's *new*."

She glided towards him, smoothing her skirts with a smile. "I have a mirror, darling. And it informed me—quite bluntly—that I look exquisite in this colour. Honestly, it's a wonder I bore you at all with taste this impeccable."

He snorted under his breath. "And what fresh disaster are you planning, dressed like that? A third husband? A revolution?"

"Well," she purred, "that depends on what eligible creatures

Yorkshire has to offer. But rest assured, Elias, I refuse to sit in this mausoleum while you play landlord and bachelor monk. One of us, at least, ought to live."

Elias dragged a hand down his face. "God help Yorkshire."

"Don't be dramatic, darling. I'm here to help." She moved to the window with graceful detachment, too graceful for a woman not up to something. After a pause, she announced airily, "There's a cheese-rolling and sheep-blessing festival in the village this weekend. I plan to attend."

Elias froze and stared at her like she'd grown antlers. "*Why?*"

She turned, innocent as sin. "Why not? There will be local refreshment, music, amusement."

"Amusement," Elias echoed.

"Besides," she added, examining her reflection in the glass with mild satisfaction, "you must be seen; people are taking notice of your restoration efforts. And the flower festival in Harrogate is the following week. I think it would do you good to accompany me."

Elias pinched the bridge of his nose. "You want me to parade through a market, watch drunk men bat wooden balls across a field with questionable technique, and sniff chrysanthemums?"

"Precisely," she replied, unbothered. "And you'll look dashing while doing it. Harrogate has no shortage of shops to assist. You can buy proper cravats—perhaps not stained with brick dust. And something edible besides boiled cabbage. And wine, Elias. Not vinegar. Something that won't blister the tongue. Let that be your salvation, if nothing else."

He exhaled through his teeth. "All this fuss over flowers and sheep, you must have an audience in mind."

Her mouth turned up at the corners. "I suppose you'll have to come along and find out."

Elias wasn't sure what unsettled him more, the idea of trailing his mother to a sheep festival, or the sudden flicker of curiosity that maybe he was becoming part of this place. A little less exile. A little more home.

* * *

Rookhaven village green had been overtaken. Pennants flapped in the breeze, bunting strung from tree to tree like the place had single-handedly repelled Napoleon. Stalls spilled over with pies, preserves, bolts of cloth, and at least one suspiciously lumpy barrel that claimed to be vintage cider.

Children darted underfoot with sticks and streamers, a fiddler squealed from a corner by the Spotted Hen tavern, and in the centre of it all—bleating, snorting, chewing—stood the sheep. Dozens of them. Some docile, some defiant. All very pungent.

Elias stood near the gate, arms crossed, sweeping the crowd like a man surveying a battlefield.

"So this," he muttered, "is what purgatory looks like."

"Don't be dramatic," Lady Cheverley murmured, adjusting her bonnet. "It's tradition."

"It smells like wet wool and duplicity," Elias shot back, glowering at a belligerent-looking sheep.

He lasted all of five minutes before someone shoved a tankard into his hand and barked, "Local bitter. Best thing you'll taste all day, lad."

Elias braced himself for the worst and blinked. It wasn't terrible. In fact, it was good. Deep, malty, sharp at the finish. Almost respectable. Then another hand appeared, thrusting a cube of pale cheese at him on a toothpick.

"Wensleydale," the man announced proudly. "With cranberries."

Elias eyed it like a trap, but bit down and stopped mid-chew. "I like it."

The man beamed at him, clapping him on the shoulder. "Course you do. Yer in Yorkshire now, lad."

Elias found himself cornered again, this time by Reverend Ward, who materialised at his elbow like an overzealous ghost.

"Splendid turnout," the clergyman chirped. "They're auctioning the rams at half past, and if I were you, Lord Blackstone, I'd try the chutney stall. Second table from the left. Changed my life, truly."

Elias nodded, but he hadn't caught a word beyond "splendid." His eyes were fixed on the Ashcroft stall, or more accurately, on Florence. She stood at the centre of the chaos, laughing at something a child said, the wind catching the blue ribbon in her hair and tugging it loose. Her sleeves were rolled enough to show her arms as she handed out prizes with brisk efficiency.

She wasn't the icy noble lady from the ball, or the forbidding heiress who'd sparred with him on the Wrenthorpe terrace. She was something else entirely. And to make the scene even more unbearable, some tall, earnest-looking fellow near the sheep pen caught her eye and gave a shy little wave.

Florence's mouth curved, not like the cold, razor-edged smile she'd given Elias, but warmer. Easier.

She hadn't even glanced his way. And for reasons he refused to examine, that irritated him.

"Gentlemen, gather round!" The call came from the wooden stage hastily erected beside the sheep pens. An elderly farmer stood there, grinning with the self-importance of a man about to change lives, a battered *speaking trumpet* in his hands.

"Today's trial," he bellowed, voice carrying across the green, "is a test of courage, wit, and livestock-handling skill! Any unmarried lad with a mind to impress the lasses—step right up!"

* * *

Honoria perched on a barrel with her lace fan and her habitual raised brow. "I take it this isn't part of your husband-finding initiative?" she drawled.

Florence handed a bright-eyed boy a stick of barley sugar and gave her friend a withering glance. "Certainly not—This is duty," she said evenly. "But, I *have* already chosen a suitor of special interest."

"Oh?" Honoria said, suddenly attentive.

Florence nodded toward a tall, awkward man loitering near the sheep pen, "There," she said. "He even smells faintly of grease and barley. Ideal."

His coat was neat but plainly cut, and he was crouched in the mud, fascinated by the turn of a ewe's hoof.

"Third son of the Greenwood family. They own a mill in Dewsbury. He's more interested in mechanisms and plough design than actually running cloth. Perfect. No ambition to interfere with my operations, and he likes sheep."

Honoria choked back a laugh. "Be still, my heart," she said, studying the subject in question. "You've outdone yourself. Tell me, do you plan to vet him on his fondness for manure before or after the wedding?"

Florence smiled. "Let's see if he can manage a sheep before

he even thinks of managing me."

Men were stepping forward, some eager, some dragged by their mothers, sleeves rolled, faces flushed with equal parts bravado and terror. Among them, Mr Greenwood, who tipped his cap to Florence with a shy grin.

Honoria perked up, like a cat spotting an unattended roast. "I do love a man who overestimates himself."

Greenwood stepped into the pen. The sheep considered him. And quite without warning, charged. He hadn't stood a chance. One second he was standing, the next he was flying—cravat fluttering, hat gone, arms windmilling—straight into a bale of hay.

Gasps. Laughter. Someone's terrier barked.

Florence groaned and started toward the pen. But two burly farmers were already hauling Greenwood upright, dazed, drenched, one boot missing, and bits of straw sticking out of his ginger hair.

"He'll live. But dinner? His pride will never recover," Honoria whispered.

Florence pressed her hand to her temple. He'll be in bed for a week with poultices and bandages, and his mother will claim I encouraged the theatrics.

She exhaled slowly, her gaze drifting across the green past the sheep pens, toward the judging table where a silver-plated plaque waited to be handed out for *Mechanical Innovation in Agricultural Tools*. Her father's chair stood behind it, straight-backed and weathered. Empty.

He'd judged that category every year since she was a girl. Not war. Not winter sickness. Not even the worst storms had kept him from it.

"He tried to stand this morning," she said, quieter now.

"Didn't make it far. Still asked for the wool returns, though."

Honoria followed her gaze, her brow lifting just slightly. "How is he?"

"He's—" Florence stopped herself. "He's tired. That's all."

"He's made of ledgers and stubbornness," Honoria said gently.

Florence nodded, her smile brittle. "That's what I keep telling myself."

A silence fell between them, not long, but long enough.

Then Honoria clucked her tongue. "You're down to nine supper guests. Tragic, really."

"I know," Florence murmured. She turned away, fussing with the corner of the tablecloth. "It shouldn't matter. One man. One dinner."

Honoria tilted her head. "But it does."

"Because Harrogate is in a few days," Florence snapped, sharper than intended. "And if I don't find someone, I'll have uneven seats at dinner. That's a doomed omen."

Even Honoria's fan hesitated. "Are we hunting for roses or restitution?"

"A replacement," Florence hissed through her teeth. "And he'd better be charming, manageable, unattached, and not afraid of *sheep*."

11

Chapter Eleven

Harrogate was in bloom.

The town was adorned with garlands and silk banners for the annual festival, and so were the crowd. The gentry turned out in full plumage: ladies with parasols like painted wings, gentlemen in tailored coats pretending not to preen, while the air sang with the mingled scent of roses, hot bread, and hopeful enthusiasm.

The Crown in Harrogate was modest but pleasant and smelled faintly of ale and roasted meat. Elias stood at the window of the bed-chamber, coat half off, when two familiar silhouettes emerged from a carriage below. There she was, Florence Ashcroft, skirts swishing, flanked by Honoria Wrenthorpe and a footman dragging a flurry of flower-patterned luggage.

No. Absolutely not. He was here for new cravats. Some proper soap. Possibly books. Not *her.*

Her laughter rose over the din of the street below, and he swore under his breath.

By the time he made it downstairs, his mother was already

holding court in the lounge, teacup in hand, lavender ribbons fluttering.

"I adore a coincidence," she purred, without even glancing at him.

"It's not a coincidence," Elias muttered darkly.

"Ah, fate then," she corrected, stirring her tea with deliberate elegance. "Perhaps nudging you in the right direction."

"She called me a *trespasser*," he grumbled.

Lady Cheverley's lips curved. "Romance often begins in adversity, darling. I threw a drink on your father before consenting to dinner."

"I am *not*—"

She cut him off, set her cup down and fixed him with a look that could have felled the cavalry. "Oh, stop glowering, Elias. You're in Harrogate. And I have need of you."

He blinked. "For *what*?"

She sniffed delicately and gestured at the door. "The florist refused to deliver my order unless I select the blooms myself, and I won't trudge about the tents alone like some lonely widow waiting for her next husband. And before you ask, no, I will not take the footman. He has a face like a funeral. You, at least, have *shoulders*."

Elias gave her an incredulous look. "You're blackmailing me with hydrangeas?"

"Blackmail is such an ugly word. I prefer persuasion." She smiled sweetly.

He exhaled through his nose and looked heavenward. "Mother, I have plans—"

"Yes," she cut in, rising to her feet, "and so do I. One of us will get what she wants today. Care to wager which?"

He glared at her. "Fine."

Lady Cheverley smiled victoriously. She plucked her lace gloves from the table. "I knew you'd see reason," she murmured. "And you may as well enjoy yourself, darling, tomorrow promises to be far more tedious."

"Tomorrow?"

"The theatre, of course." She said, already halfway to the door. "Everyone who is anyone in Harrogate will be there. Wear something devastating. It never hurts to remind them who you were born to be."

He groaned. "Perfect. Another evening of polite applause and dull conversation."

She paused, one hand on the doorframe, glancing back slyly. "Not if you're seated near Miss Ashcroft, it won't."

He muttered darkly, and she carried on as though his temper were no more threatening than a drizzle on the moors.

* * *

Harrogate Theatre was alive with flickering lights and rustling silk. The chandeliers dripped crystal, the orchestra swelled, and the audience swayed with the collective attentiveness bred from habit rather than interest.

Elias hadn't followed the performance. He couldn't recall a single line. Instead, he'd watched *them.* Florence Ashcroft and Honoria Wrenthorpe occupied a box high enough to look down on everyone. They whispered behind their fans, heads dipped together with conspiratorial grins. Not once did they glance at the stage or bother to applaud.

Around him, debutantes clapped delicately, eyes darting sideways to gauge which gentlemen noticed. Fans fluttered in choreographed patterns. There were blushes on cue, laughter where appropriate, and posture straight from a finishing school primer.

But not Florence. She leaned closer to Honoria, murmured something, and both of them stifled laughter—at someone else's expense, he was certain. She didn't perform for anyone. Didn't try to charm the room. She didn't need to.

When her gaze swept the theatre again, it caught on him. Her fan stilled mid-flutter. Her spine lifted, just a fraction. She met his eyes squarely, and the surrounding theatre dissolved into little more than noise and movement. For a breath or two, they held each other's stare, and there was nothing polite about it. Hers was a challenge wrapped in calm. His was a warning wrapped in fascination.

The curtain fell, severing the moment like a blade. Florence moved first, fan snapping shut as if the matter were settled. Honoria followed close behind, still smiling, though at what, Elias couldn't guess. It didn't matter. He was already rising.

The intermission spilled into the foyer in a flurry of impatient gentlemen jostling for lemonade or a discreet brandy. Elias moved with them, not by intention but instinct. By the time he reached the refreshment table, she was there, hand poised.

"I see the lemonade has survived the masses," Elias said, low and dry, stepping into the space beside them as though it belonged to him.

Honoria blinked in surprise. "Oh! Lord Blackstone. Would you—?"

"I'll fetch it," he said, already stepping forward.

"No." Florence's voice cut clean through the crowd. Sharp enough to draw a few curious glances.

His hand stilled. "No?" he repeated, loud enough for her to hear the bite under it.

She didn't flinch. "we're perfectly capable of securing our own lemonade, my lord. Thank you."

For a moment, he stood motionless, the faint scent of roses and citrus hanging between them.

Honoria coughed into her glove, clearly enjoying herself. "Well," she murmured, "this is... *fun*."

Florence stepped back. Dismissing him like a servant she'd finished with.

"Good evening, my lord," she said, her voice as cool and level as her gaze.

Elias dipped his head. "Miss Ashcroft."

She turned. Her fan resumed its idle flutter as she slipped into the crowd with Honoria, the moment already discarded.

He watched her go. Longer than he should have. Every movement precise, indifferent. Except he didn't quite believe it.

At the far end of the foyer, a flash of violet silk caught his eye. Lady Cheverley stood by the far doors, head tilted in a familiar angle of amused appraisal, speaking to a gentleman Elias didn't recognise.

Well-dressed, a little too polished, leaning in close. She laid one gloved hand on his forearm, laughing at something he said as though they were the only two people in the theatre.

Elias's brow furrowed. There had been no trace of her this morning. She usually sat embroidering in the lounge, fortified by tea, toast, and unsolicited opinions on his posture, future, and lack of decent collars. He'd peered around the breakfast room. Empty. A quick word with the innkeeper had revealed she'd stepped out around dawn with a "gentleman companion."

Elias didn't ask further. He didn't want to *know* further.

It wasn't simply the man that bothered him. It was the memory of London's drawing rooms gone silent when she entered. The way her laughter, too loud and too careless, had lingered in gossip long after she'd left. How every whispered remark about her became a stone hung around *his* neck.

And now here she was again. Playing the same game, as though history had taught her nothing. As though it were *his* duty to rebuild their name while she tore it down, one indiscretion at a time.

Perhaps Yorkshire would be kinder than London. Perhaps the locals would chalk her flirtations up to eccentricity rather than disgrace.

But staring at her now, leaning onto some stranger's arm as though excitement were her birthright, Elias doubted it.

12

Chapter Twelve

Harrogate's streets were shedding the last of the morning mist when Elias stepped into the pale light, collar up against the chill, a headache pressing behind his eyes.

A few early risers bustled between bakeries and market stalls. As he crossed the cobbles, the gleam of painted letters caught him mid-step.

Gibson & Finch, Booksellers. Rare, Useful, and Curious Titles Since 1782.

Volumes filled the windows, some so old the spines looked ready to crumble. *Five minutes*, he told himself. He pushed the door open, and the bell above chimed—

"Of course it's you." Her voice stopped him mid-step. Florence Ashcroft, a book already tucked under her arm. Her maid sat primly by the door, wearing the expression of someone who had long since run out of patience.

Elias's gaze travelled over her. "You're everywhere."

She raised a brow, as though he'd proven her point about something she hadn't even voiced yet.

"And yet, somehow, always exactly where I'm supposed to be. You, however…" she let her eyes wash over him, "…seem lost."

He stepped inside and let the door shut behind him. "I was under the impression Harrogate was *public*."

"Is *that* what you tell the women you follow into bookshops?"

"I was *following* cravats," he said. "This is a diversion."

Elias exhaled through his nose and glanced at the shelves to his left. "Perhaps you'd prefer we keep to opposite sides. For the sake of harmony."

"I think that's wise." She drifted to the far wall, spine straight, fingertips grazing the leather spines as though the books ought to be grateful for her attention. She moved with the same unbothered command she brought to everything else, which only made her harder to ignore.

Every time she moved, he was aware of it. The faint rustle of her skirts, the soft *thwack* of a book closed a little too firmly. When he reached for a volume on flora, she was already glancing up from behind a stack of atlases with that infuriatingly judicious look. He stayed there longer than necessary to prove he could.

She stepped toward the counter with a book under her arm. He followed, though if pressed, he'd have insisted it was because he'd finished.

Florence glanced down at the books in his hands:

Valeting for Gentlemen: A Complete Manual.

The Layman's Guide to Yorkshire's Moorland, Flora, and Fauna.

She blinked. "You surprise me, Lord Blackstone."

"Flattered," he said, not bothering to look at her.

"Don't be. I assumed you couldn't read."

That earned her his attention. "Tell me, Miss Ashcroft," he said mildly, "is mockery your preferred form of affection?"

"I wouldn't know," she said, passing her book to the shopkeeper. "I've never needed to fake either."

They lingered at the counter while the shopkeeper wrapped their books, his hands slow, the string taking forever to knot.

Her fingers brushed his, a whisper of contact through the gloves. Florence looked at him with something unreadable in her eyes.

His chest tightened under her scrutiny.

The shopkeeper cleared his throat.

Florence stepped back with perfect composure. "Enjoy your moorland," she murmured, as she turned, her skirts catching on his boots defiantly.

He watched her leave and told himself to let her win. But his feet, traitorous as ever, carried him after her anyway. Falling into step outside, he nodded toward the tearoom across the street. "Would you allow me to buy you a cup of something vaguely palatable?"

Florence glanced sidelong at him. "With all of Harrogate watching?"

Elias met her gaze, unblinking. "Let them."

She gave a soft, scoffing breath, but her eyes didn't leave his. "Given your reputation," she added dryly, "I daresay we'll both be married off by breakfast."

He chuckled low in his throat. "If the scandal papers are to be believed, I've already buried three wives and shot a bishop."

Her brow rose. "Only one bishop?"

"The others were armed." He shrugged, amused. "I promise not to elope with you. Not before cake, at least."

That earned him something unexpected, a flash of warmth she didn't bother to disguise.

"Fine," she said. "But only because my maid won't stop sighing at me if I faint from thirst."

They sat in a quiet corner of the tearoom, beneath faded floral wallpaper, with her maid positioned at a discreet distance. Elias, cautious but genuinely curious, asked her opinion on mill expansion. Florence, surprised but unwilling to waste the opportunity, offered it.

Somewhere between insults and industry, they discovered they shared the same quiet, stubborn craving—not for peace, not for romance, but for purpose.

He stirred his tea, "You surprise me, Miss Ashcroft. I'd assumed you held me in the same regard as a loaded pistol."

"You are a loaded pistol, my lord." Her voice calm and unflinching. "I just haven't decided where you're aimed."

He looked at her then—not with flirtation, but with something sharper. "Is that your own observation… or someone else's?"

"They say many things. A duel. A scandal. A woman. Or a debt—you left London rather suddenly."

His fingers curled loosely around his cup. "It's funny how people prefer stories over facts."

"You won't deny it?"

"Would it matter if I did?"

She tilted her head, eyes narrowing. "I don't care for gossip. But I do care for patterns. And yours suggests a man who runs when things catch fire."

"Do you behave like this with every man in Yorkshire?" he

asked, watching her over the rim of his cup.

Her eyes flicked to his steadily. "Only the ones I invite to dinner."

That stopped him cold. "I'm sorry—what?"

She set her cup down with infuriating composure. "Friday. Supper. At Ashcroft Manor. We're hosting a small gathering to discuss community investment and industry initiatives—apprenticeships, machinery innovation, trade schools. That sort of thing."

He blinked. "A dinner… for mill reform?"

"A supper for the future," she corrected. "Father's idea, mostly—he used to hold these every year, invite the more forward-thinking landowners and factory owners to scheme over pudding. We've revived it this year. Quietly."

Elias hesitated, then gave a slow nod. "My father used to speak of those. Said they were the only dinners worth attending, no card games, just blueprints and arguments."

Her lips twitched. "The rules are simple: no egos, no idle hands, and no speeches longer than three minutes."

Elias found himself at a loss.

Florence sipped her tea, unbothered, as though she hadn't turned the entire conversation upside down.

He studied her, trying to decide if she was serious, if she was mocking him, or if—God help him—*both*.

At the tearoom door, Florence gave him one last cool, unreadable glance before turning away, her maid in tow.

Elias watched her go, then stepped out into the damp Harrogate air, his thoughts louder than the chatter of the street. By the time he returned to The Crown, dusk was already settling, and the streets were emptying.

The door to his chamber creaked shut as he stepped into the

dim stillness. A fire smouldered low in the grate. Elias tossed his gloves onto the sideboard and sat heavily on the edge of the bed. The headboard groaned as he leaned back, elbows on his thighs. He wasn't thinking of Florence.

Not deliberately. But the image came anyway, the way she looked in the morning light, gaze turned to the window, lost in thought. A little too sharp for comfort. A little too beautiful to ignore.

Their tea room conversation had caught him off guard.

They'd spoken like two people who had almost forgotten how. He could still hear her laughter—low, unexpected—and see the mischief that sparked behind those dark eyes. She'd bested him in every exchange, left him disarmed, and somehow wanting more.

When she'd asked about the duel, she hadn't flinched.

No coy glances. No false outrage. No attempt to charm her way to the truth.

She'd simply looked at him, unbothered, and waited.

He hadn't answered. Not really. Just another polished deflection, the kind he'd given a hundred times before to people who only wanted gossip dressed as concern.

She'd nodded, calm and deliberate, like she'd expected nothing more. Let silence carry the weight of the question, as if that alone told her what she needed to know.

What left him oddly breathless as he sat there in the dim, fire-warmed quiet—was that she didn't flinch from the man he had been, didn't try to invent the man he ought to be.

And in a life filled with punishment and performance, that felt like something dangerously close to grace.

* * *

The scent of peat smoke, Maud's baking, and old floor polish wrapped around him the moment he stepped inside the Hall. Rain had come while he was away, slicking the flagstones and sinking back into the bones of the old place. He peeled off his gloves, handed his coat to a startled maid, and called for Tom.

The young lad appeared at a slight jog, waistcoat skewed, and a smudge of ink on his thumb. "My lord?"

Elias held out a neatly wrapped parcel. "For you."

Tom studied the worn leather volume. Valeting for Gentlemen: A Complete Manual.

"Sir?"

"You'll need it. Frankly, so will I."

Tom turned it over in his hands as if it might vanish. "No one's ever given me a book before."

Elias exhaled, something between amusement and resignation. "Chapter three covers laundry and starching."

Tom looked up, beaming. "I'll read it tonight, sir. Thank you. Truly."

Elias allowed himself a faint smile as he turned on his heel. "See that you do. And stop turning my cravats into laundry mishaps I have to wear around my neck."

Outside, he caught sight of Calder trudging across the rear grounds in boots older than sin, Jed trotting faithfully at his heels. At the sight of Elias, the old man straightened, doffing his cap with a nod. "Mornin', m'lord."

Elias surveyed the stretch of land behind the house, hands behind his back. He'd spent weeks hunched over his father's ledgers, half the notes written in a hand he barely remembered. There was little magic in it, just columns of losses and repairs his father never made. But reading it felt like walking old paths, ones he'd known as a boy and forgotten as a man. "How much of this is ours?"

"To the bend, in't stream," Calder replied. "East field borders Ashcroft land."

Elias folded his arms, gaze narrowing. "And if we had labourers, proper drainage, fencing, what could we make of it?"

Calder blinked at him, caught off guard. "Well, we could bring t'orchard back," he drawled. "Run some sheep, maybe. Perhaps a kitchen garden that don't taste of bog."

Elias nodded. "I want a plan. Costs, materials, and the number of hands you'd need. On my desk by the end of the week."

Calder scratched his head and gave a toothy grin. "Aye, m'lord. I'll draw summat up. See if we can't make summat of it all." He turned back toward the stables, already muttering to himself about frost lines and plough teams. Elias watched him go; he let his gaze drift to the dark line of moor beyond the house. His father would have called it drudgery, too busy chasing politics and patronage. Elias found it oddly satisfying, this sense of building something wholly his. It wasn't instinct. It was work, and it was learning. But for the first time in years, he wanted to.

Elias had sworn he wouldn't rot in Yorkshire. But now he found himself eager for growth.

13

Chapter Thirteen

Ashcroft Manor hummed with preparation. Platters gleamed, crystal caught the light, and decanters stood at attention. The air in the parlour was thick with beeswax and quiet rebellion.

"A tally of faults and virtues?" Honoria arched a brow across the table, a spoon of blackberry syllabub suspended midway to her lips.

Florence nodded, eyes precise as pins as she finalised the seating plan. "Secret, of course. We're not savages."

"We are, however, selecting your future husband like he's a prize ram at market."

Florence gave a crisp nod. "Indeed. I need a husband. Not a romance." She tapped her pencil against the guest list. "Tonight, I test their character, or find the flaws they've tried to hide."

Honoria leaned over to read the parchment. "'Maternal Interference,' 'Public Scandal Potential,' *'Immoderate ardour'*—Florence!"

Florence didn't even look up. "I refuse to be chased down corridors by a man desperate to secure an heir before breakfast."

"No first sons, then?"

"The burden of legacy makes them insufferable." She crossed off Lord Fairbanks with a decisive stroke. "Second or third sons only. No ambition to meddle in mills, or run mine."

"But they could still be interested in you," Honoria said.

Florence paused. "They can have mistresses, if it's discreet. I need only freedom."

Honoria sipped her tea, watching her over the rim of the cup, blue eyes glinting.

"Then why, pray, did you invite Lord Blackstone?"

Florence's fingers tightened on the pencil until the lead threatened to snap, her breath catching once before she forced it steady. "It was… expedient."

Honoria set down her cup with deliberate grace, her tone maddeningly mild. "Was it? Only, he doesn't appear on your tally. Not anywhere."

Florence straightened the parchment, her knuckles whitening. "He doesn't need to be. He isn't a serious candidate."

Honoria leaned back, tapping a finger against the arm of her chair, a knowing smile playing at her lips.

"Yet in Harrogate, he asked you about your engineering interests."

Florence's pencil paused mid-scratch, her breath catching. "He was being polite."

"Polite enough to quote your father's pamphlet on hydraulic weirs?"

The faintest flush crept up Florence's neck. "That doesn't matter."

Honoria's triumphant smile deepened. "You like him."

Florence's eyes flicked up long enough to glare. "I don't want to like him. That's the problem. He's dangerous. And entirely wrong for what I need."

Honoria tilted her head, her pale curls brushing her cheek. "Because he understands you?"

Florence stared at the page, her voice barely above a whisper. "No. Because he wouldn't… disappear. Not the way I'd need him to. And he'd never accept the kind of marriage I'm willing to offer."

The room fell quiet, the only sound the faint tick of the clock. After a full minute, Florence folded the parchment with finality.

"Tonight, we cut the field in half. Five left standing. Then I take the measure of each, individually."

Honoria covered her mouth with her hand, though her grin peeked through. "Shall I fetch a bell to announce the bouts?"

Florence's smile thinned. "This is courtship, Honoria. Not boxing."

"Are you sure?" Honoria drawled, fanning herself. "Because I'm certain Lord Blackstone is hoping for a rematch."

Florence gathered the placecards into a neat pile, her fingers unsteady for a heartbeat before she composed herself. She cast a glance down the hallway toward her father's dark study. A pang twisted behind her ribs. The man who built half of Rookhaven could no longer climb a single stair without coughing up blood. And still, he worried about her future more than his own.

"Let's hope," she murmured. "He's not foolish enough to make it past round one." But already, she was worried he might.

* * *

Elias had rarely felt so out of place in a drawing room. Which was absurd, he was one of the wealthiest men in the county, seated in one of its grandest houses, wearing a cravat that had once earned praise from a duchess. And yet, as his gaze swept the room—ten men, two women, and enough tension to snap a loomstring, something felt wrong.

This wasn't the forum he'd been promised. He took a measured sip of wine, letting his gaze drift. A few of the others seemed equally unsettled; one sent him a puzzled look across the hearth, another kept glancing toward the door as though reinforcements might arrive.

He'd expected charts, discussions of apprenticeship schemes, perhaps a spirited argument about mechanical threshers. Instead, he found starched collars, polite flattery, and the distinct smell of ambition.

Every man in the room was eligible. Well-dressed. Well-placed. Smiling a little too hard in Florence Ashcroft's direction.

And Florence? She was radiant, gliding from guest to guest—not with flirtation, but with control. The footmen moved like clockwork, refilling glasses before they were half-empty, while conversation floated around him, all polite laughter and the depth of a puddle.

Florence was laughing in the far corner, her hand resting on the arm of some bespectacled bore who looked more enamoured with his own voice than her.

There were three gentlemen clustered near her, clearly acquainted, and far too comfortable in her presence for his liking. One of them—Layton, wasn't it?—was gesturing animatedly, glasses slipping down his nose, talking some nonsense about public sanitation like it was poetry. Florence leaned in, listening with genuine interest.

Of course, she would like him. Earnest. Educated. No known duels.

Even Honoria was watching, lounging near the mantel like a cat, scribbling something on a folded scrap of parchment and tucking it into her fan.

Elias forced himself into small talk with the nearest group of men. A banker's son droned on about the price of cotton and his new carriage. Another laughed like a braying mule and did it far too often. He caught stray snippets of conversation swirling around the room.

"My estate manager swears by peat..."

"I had to let the footman go—disgraceful conduct..."

"She's an admirable horsewoman, wouldn't you say?"

That last remark made something in him twist. The idea of Florence being dissected like a thoroughbred at auction set his teeth on edge.

The dinner chime saved him, or so he thought. The dining room was candlelit and polished, every piece of silverware glinting with promise. Until he saw the seating arrangement, he muttered a curse under his breath. Exiled to the far end of the table, he watched Florence claim the centre, flanked on either side, untouchable. For a brief, wicked moment, he considered feigning a fall from his chair to disrupt the tableau.

The soup was tolerable, but the pheasant was dry.

The man opposite him was insufferable, a ruddy-faced industrialist's son who had made his first thousand in railway shares and spoke with the subtlety of a siege. "You see, Lord Blackstone," the man boomed, sloshing Claret close to the pristine tablecloth, "the key to financial success is speculation. It's the future, you know. One simply *must* take risks."

Elias gave him a thin, wintry smile. "And I suppose the poor must take the consequences."

The man guffawed, missing the point.

Halfway through dessert, Elias caught Honoria scribbling again. Another mark. Another flick of her fan. Was she keeping count?

Florence remained at the centre, leaning toward her companions as though she cared about their dull little confessions.

He drained his Port in one swallow, the stem of the glass biting into his fingers. His temper coiled tighter with every smile she offered someone else.

By the time the last course was cleared, he could feel himself at the brink. One more laugh from her in another man's direction and he might—well—something he'd later regret. Elias didn't waste any time. He rose and let the screech of his chair legs stretch enough to draw a few glances. She didn't even look up, still nodding at whatever inanity her neighbour was offering.

He inclined his head to the nearest footman, muttered something about needing air, and strode out into the hall. Better the cold than watching her simper.

There were three doors, two stern-faced portraits, one snuffed candle, and the faintest sound of soft footsteps retreating toward the drawing room.

Honoria Wrenthorpe. Perfect.

He caught up with her as she reached for the decanter of Ratafia on the sideboard.

She froze, her fingers faltering, the liquid sloshing into the tray before she righted it.

"Miss Wrenthorpe," Elias said smoothly, though even to his ears it sounded more like a warning than a greeting.

Honoria blinked up at him, her expression polite but tense, as though she'd been cornered.

"Lord Blackstone."

"May I?" he asked, already pouring a measure before she could answer. "You've been attentive this evening."

"Attentive?" she echoed, voice an octave higher than necessary.

He leaned one shoulder against the wall, gaze steady, voice mild enough to make her shift her weight. "Your little fan. Not merely decorative, is it? Or has some new fashion begun—ladies of quality marking out their dinner guests?"

Honoria stiffened, the colour rising to her cheeks. "I beg your pardon?"

His voice dropped a notch, soft and deliberate. "I saw the marks. Counted ten men. Miss Ashcroft. And you. Twelve. Curious arithmetic, unless one is keeping a tally."

Honoria tried to meet his gaze. "I think you've misread the—"

"I think," Elias cut in, "I have *not*. It's an odd balance for a conversation about apprenticeships."

"You think it strange?" she asked, with forced lightness.

"Curious," he corrected.

Silence fell, broken only by the faint crackle of the hearth.

At last, she exhaled, her eyes still on the decanter. "It was only something to pass the time. Nothing more."

"Is that what this is?" Elias murmured, swirling the Ratafia in his glass, eyes fixed on her. "Amusement?"

Honoria looked away. "No. Not… exactly. She's trying to be—practical. Doing what she always does, thinking ahead."

Elias studied her, the edges of her words catching on something sharp. "Ahead to what?"

Her fingers tightened around her glass. "That's not mine to say." The fire gave a soft snap behind them, its warmth at odds with the sudden chill beneath her words. From the hall, the faint sounds of conversation were too far off to hear clearly, too close to ignore.

Thinking ahead.

He straightened, with the prickling sense that he'd missed something important. This wasn't *just* supper. It was something else.

He'd walked straight into the middle of a strategy, wearing his best boots, expecting blueprints, and now seated among men who looked like they thought the prize might be Florence herself.

"So then," Elias murmured, "which poor fool has she chosen to saddle herself with?"

Honoria stilled. He could see the shift, even in his periphery. the tension in her shoulders, the quiet struggle not to betray Florence. Not to flinch.

When she finally spoke, her voice was level, but the effort showed.

"Someone… less complicated."

That earned a quiet, sardonic laugh. He drained the last of his glass and set it down with precision.

"No," he said. "I'd already guessed as much."

She hesitated, then offered, "She isn't looking for love, Lord Blackstone. She's looking for safe. A name that shields her, not one that challenges everything she builds."

He glanced at her, cold flashing behind his eyes. "And I'm a threat to that?"

Honoria looked down at the fan in her hands. "You're… a variable. She didn't expect you. And Florence doesn't like what she can't control."

That cut deeper than he expected. He stood there, feeling the weight of it settle, hot and unwelcome. "Well then," he said coldly, "she'd better learn to revise her calculations."

Without waiting for her reply, Elias turned on his heel and strode back toward the dining room, his blood simmering, and Florence Ashcroft, damn her, more alluring than ever.

14

Chapter Fourteen

Florence kicked off her slippers with more venom than necessary. "They were ghastly," she declared, collapsing inelegantly onto the velvet chaise.

"You invited them," Honoria replied, not looking up as she shuffled parchment across the escritoire. "One can hardly blame the rats for the state of the cheese."

"I was hoping for eccentric," Florence snapped, "not insufferable. Is that too much to ask?"

Honoria only hummed, uncorked the ink, and dipped her quill with deliberate calm. "Let's begin. Name, offence, elimination. No clemency."

Florence straightened, chin lifting. "Agreed."

They began.

Mr Worthing—dull as tepid tea. Eliminated.

Sir Oswald-Penn—said nevertheless five times in one sentence. Eliminated.

Mr Cavendish—overly fixated on his mother's corgi. Eliminated.

Captain Renshaw—roving eyes, smelled faintly of absinthe.

Eliminated with prejudice.

It continued until Honoria paused, quill poised, a faint curve at the corner of her mouth. Without looking up, she murmured: "Well. That leaves six. Shall I strike Lord Blackstone from the parchment now, or would you prefer the honour?"

Florence's foot froze mid-swing. "What? Why?"

Honoria glanced up, expression all innocence. "Because you said quite emphatically, if I recall, that he was not a proper candidate. Also, he glared at three different men during dinner. And made the entire table nervous."

Florence folded her arms. "He doesn't glare. He... watches. Like a predator. It's just his face."

"Oh yes," Honoria murmured, eyes glinting as she tapped her chin. "His very handsome face."

Florence ignored that. "Besides, he wasn't the worst conversationalist."

"He hardly spoke," Honoria countered.

"Precisely," Florence replied crisply. "It was... novel."

Honoria arched a brow. "You're keeping him because he didn't bore you senseless?"

Florence adjusted the place-cards before her with unnecessary precision, her fingers lingering longer than necessary over lord Blackstone's name.

"It's as good a reason as any. And I need a sound selection."

"Of course," Honoria murmured, lips curving as she re-wrote the suitor's names, with lord Blackstone's name larger than the rest. "And what a coincidence that your selection includes the only man who's made you visibly breathless."

Florence stilled, colour rising. "He does not—I am not—"

Honoria, still smiling, reached across, picked up the place-cards, with exaggerated care, and crossed out 'Mr Taverley' instead. "Well then. He stays."

Florence narrowed her eyes. "You are meddling. And I won't have it."

"Meddle?" Honoria's eyes flicked down to the parchment, her thumb brushing over Blackstone's name as though smoothing it into place. "I won't meddle. I'll… nudge."

Florence let out a theatrical sigh. "Fine. We're down to five. "

Honoria turned over a fresh sheet of parchment, quill at the ready. "The Prendhurst Ball is next week. The perfect opportunity, dozens of ways to test wit, stamina, and rhythm."

Florence's eyes narrowed. "Stamina?"

"Strictly on the dance floor," Honoria said primly.

Florence tried and failed not to smile.

Honoria leaned in, her eyes gleaming now, her voice dropping. "We'll cut them to three that night. Let everyone else assume it's courtship by candlelight. But we'll know better." She tapped her nose lightly with the quill. "Bout two, in the game of husbands."

Florence stood, stretching her arms overhead as though she could shake off the evening's tension. "It's a good thing Lord Blackstone doesn't know," she murmured. "He'd never agree to be judged like that."

Honoria's eyes lowered to the parchment as she straightened the place-cards and, without a word, placed lord Blackstone's name at the top.

* * *

Tom fumbled with the collar pin.

"Careful," Elias muttered, lifting his chin. "This is the only shirt I have left that isn't frayed to hell."

"Of course, my lord," Tom said, fingers still trembling. "It's—the starch—"

"The starch didn't dress me. *You* did. Are you always this nervous, or is it just me?"

Tom's ears turned pink. "I—only slightly more with you, my lord."

Elias sighed and shrugged out of his coat himself, dropping it unceremoniously over the nearest chair.

Tom gave a panicked little gasp and darted forward. "I'll press it immediately—"

"Let it die with dignity," Elias said, moving to the mirror. He studied the tinted scrap around his neck. "Is this... lavender?"

Tom froze, hands still hovering over the abandoned coat. "Only *a little,* my lord. Perhaps lilac in poor light."

"It was white less than a week ago."

"Yes, my lord. But I believe one of the maids used a basin that had contained—"

"Let me guess," Elias cut in, loosening his cuffs. "Dried petals and optimism."

Tom coughed discreetly.

Elias tugged the cravat loose with quick, practised fingers. "No wonder that loudmouth across from me wouldn't stop smirking. I've spent the evening looking like a bloody spring-time debutante."

Tom ventured a weak chuckle. "I thought it rather suited you, my lord."

Elias turned, shirt already unbuttoned to the waist, fixing him with a cool stare. "Tom."

"My lord?"

"Why are you agreeing with everything I say?"

Tom straightened, visibly summoning courage. "Because, my lord, that's what valets do. Chapter One of *The Modern Gentleman's Gentleman's Guide,* 'Harmony in the Household: The Valet's Duty to Defer.'"

Elias raised his brows. "Is that so?"

Tom nodded. "It says—and I quote—'A true valet anticipates all things, questions nothing, and steadfastly supports the master's judgement even when it is foolish.'"

Elias looked at him.

Tom smiled nervously.

"You've read the book?"

"Cover to cover. Twice."

"Burn it."

Tom's face fell. "But it's—"

"Utter rot. From now on, you'll speak plainly to me. That's an order."

Tom hesitated. "Even if I think you're wrong, my lord?"

"Especially then."

Tom wet his lips, "Well, sir… that waistcoat does make you look a bit like a wedding cake."

Elias blinked before barking a laugh. "There's the lad I hired."

Tom grinned, straightening a little.

"Good. Now help me find the bottle of brandy I left somewhere under that pile of good intentions I had earlier. And if you ever hand me another lavender cravat, I'll have you catalogue every portrait in the attic. In Latin."

"Yes, my lord."

A pause.

"That was a joke, Tom."

"Of course, my lord. I'll brush up on my declensions. Just in case."

Elias rubbed his temples, muttering under his breath. "God preserve me from competence."

The fire in the hearth had dwindled to a sullen glow, the sort of light that couldn't warm a teacup, let alone his thoughts. Elias sat back in the worn armchair by the window, brandy glass tilted idly in his hand.

Somewhere down the hall, no doubt, Tom was alphabetising pomades or trying to scrub lavender out of linen. And here he sat, in the dark, replaying every word Miss Wrenthorpe hadn't quite meant to give away.

She wants a husband in name only.

The thought had lodged itself in his skull like a splinter. Florence had smiled, that awful little smile that said she was in control, and he was nothing more than a name to fill a place at her table.

"Name only," he muttered aloud, swirling the brandy. "What the hell does that mean?"

It meant some dull-eyed baronet who spoke in monotone and didn't mind being banished to the library while his wife ran her empire. It meant no heirs. No legacy. No real companionship, merely the illusion of stability.

Ludicrous. And yet the idea of her offering that arrangement to someone else—someone who wasn't him—unsettled him more than he liked.

Worse still… He didn't hate the idea of being the one she'd choose.

The thought struck hard, enough to pull a breath through his teeth. Elias shifted forward in the chair, elbows to knees, as if he could physically outrun it.

Florence Ashcroft? Content with silence and solitude, with polite disinterest?

Boredom would overwhelm her within a month. Unless that was the plan. Marry someone so painfully uninspiring that no one would even notice his absence. A man so beige the *ton* would thank her for keeping him out of their sight.

Elias frowned into the dying fire.

She had spark. He'd seen it at the village festival, laughing with the children, wiping flour from a boy's nose as she handed him a sweet. The way she'd scooped up a runaway lamb like she'd done it every Sunday.

And she didn't want children?

He shifted in his chair, unsettled now—not physically, but somewhere deeper. Somewhere worse.

Why was he thinking about her at all? Did it matter if she married some sop who could barely string two words together?

Why did it grind in his chest like a pebble in a boot?

He sipped his brandy, watching the light catch in the amber like it might hold an answer.

Maybe it was because she looked at him like he was the most infuriating man she'd ever met. Or maybe—God help him—it was because she *challenged* him, and she never once looked at him with pity.

She argued, teased, even scowled. But never pity. And that made her dangerous. Because now he was starting to wonder what it would be like if she smiled at him the way she smiled at those she cared for, if she touched his hand with the same affection she gave her friend.

He set the brandy down, harder than he meant to. *What the hell is wrong with you, Blackstone?*

You didn't come here to start losing your head over a woman.

You came to Yorkshire to repair your name, not ruin it over a woman who rides astride, provokes you at every turn, and runs a supper like a military campaign. You need a wife who will stay at Mooredge quietly, who will smooth over your scandal without adding to it. Someone old money, well-bred, discreet, someone like Miss Wrenthorpe. His gaze drifted to the black stretch of moor beyond the window, where frost already glinted on the glass.

And yet.

15

Chapter Fifteen

Elias speared his eggs as though they'd personally offended him.

Across from him, his mother flourished.

Cheeks flushed from the fire, dark curls immaculate, plum silk gown daringly inappropriate for half-mourning. A queen in exile.

"The tradesmen," she chirped, pouring tea with infuriating grace, "have worked wonders already. The west wing may even be habitable by Christmastide."

Elias grunted into his toast. "If one enjoys blight and rattling windows," he muttered.

She carried on unheeded. "And Mrs Vale tells me we've had three new footmen apply this week. The news is spreading. A family of stature restored to Mooredge.

That sort of thing tends to stir excitement."

"I'm not interested in stirring anything," he muttered, "except my tea."

She regarded him intently over the rim of her cup. "Nevertheless," she remarked affably, "your attendance at Miss

Ashcroft's supper was noted."

That earned her his full attention.

"Miss Ashcroft strikes me as a most capable young woman. Unconventional, yes, but one must make allowances for northern peculiarities." She smiled.

Elias's teeth clenched. "I wasn't aware supper with ten gentlemen and two ladies qualified as *peculiar*. I'd have called it strategic."

"Indeed," she said, dabbing her lips. "You've always admired women with a bit of wit about them."

His fork paused mid-air. "Mother."

She pressed on, undeterred. "Will she be at the Prendhurst's ball, do you think? I imagine the Wrenthorpe girl will also be there. Poor child, her mother's desperation is practically stitched into the hem of her gowns."

"Is there a reason," Elias said slowly, "you've taken such a sudden and intimate interest in my social calendar?"

"Oh, darling, don't be absurd. I've always been interested—I've always had more pressing matters until now." Her smile thinned. "But you're settling in. A little effort, a few engagements, and perhaps you'll even find a reason to stay." She paused then, eyes lingering on him longer than usual, weighing something. "Robert would've liked that," she said, almost idly, eyes on the fire. "You always had his sense of integrity. Not your father's sharp edges." She took another sip of tea, as if she hadn't said something suspiciously close to affection.

"You mean besides playing landlord to a crumbling ruin and *supervising tradesmen like a governess?*"

She gave a very particular shrug, the kind that looked casual, but was anything but. "You may find Yorkshire more tolerable with a wife."

His laughter was barbed and humourless. "You sound like the matrons we escaped in Mayfair."

"And yet you invited Miss Ashcroft to a teahouse in Harrogate last week."

His brow furrowed. "I did not *invite* Florence Ashcroft to—"

"I beg to differ," she interjected, with a dismissive flick of her wrist, as her bracelets chimed. "At the theatre, you offered her lemonade. You accepted her supper invitation. You laughed with her in a tearoom, Elias. That counts."

He shook his head. "You'd rather talk about me than admit what you're doing."

Her lips curved into something far too knowing. "Oh, Elias. How suspicious you are."

"You," he said. "And your concern about my romantic prospects. When you're clearly busy enough with your own social calendar."

Her smile held, but turned brittle. "Don't be ridiculous."

"Then why," Elias prodded, easing back in his chair, "are you repeating old patterns?"

She stilled, her expression giving nothing away. Calmly and carefully, she stirred her tea. "Your distaste for being managed has always been apparent," she murmured.

"I hate it more," he said, "when it works."

The fire crackled behind them, a counterpoint to the heavy silence in the room.

"Is it someone I know?" Elias asked, more gently now.

"No." Her voice was quiet. "And it's not serious."

Not yet, he heard in her pause. She looked up swiftly, the glint back in her eyes. "But I'd advise you to think seriously, Elias. The estate is waking. People are watching. You'll need an ally here."

"I already have one," he said."His name is Calder, and he is certainly capable of defending this estate."

His mother sniffed. "A grumpy groundsman and a deaf spaniel do not a legacy make."

Elias smiled. "You've never seen them chase off a drunk poacher."

She didn't smile back.

* * *

The Prendhurst estate was ablaze with lanterns, every window aglow as if determined to outshine the moon. Merriment spilled down the steps and across the gravel, accompanied by the strains of a waltz and the clink of champagne flutes.

The ballroom glittered, all gilded mouldings, polished floors, and orchestral pomp. At the far end stood Mr Prendhurst himself, stooped but smiling, basking in the evening's splendour while his much-younger wife held court with an iron fan and a smile sharpened by social ambition.

Elias surveyed the elaborately dressed crowd, his gaze settling on Florence as she moved through the set, graceful, composed, entirely at ease among them.

He recognised four of the supper guests circling her—*The shortlist,* he supposed.

Beside him, his mother took a casual sip of champagne. "She dances well," she observed mildly.

"I suppose," Elias muttered, jaw tight enough to crack enamel.

Florence twirled past on the arm of a gentleman with a chin like a shovel.

She laughed at something he said, but it lacked sincerity. This was the laugh she used when she was being watched. And Elias realised he didn't much care to see her perform for anyone but him.

He turned, spotting Honoria Wrenthorpe near the potted palms, and approached like a man who'd already decided what answer he wanted "Has she concluded the *interviews* with her prospective suitors?" he asked, skipping pleasantries.

Honoria blinked at him in surprise. "Are you inquiring about the status of *your* application?"

"My *question* was whether she had excluded me."

Honoria's mouth curved into a feline smile. "She didn't. Not properly. We granted you a reprieve. On the strength of—and you'll appreciate this—your ability to hold a civilised conversation."

"That was—" he began, scowling.

"Rare," Honoria interjected.

Her eyes twinkled, and she subtly inclined her head. "Tell me, my lord, do you intend to keep circling her like a hawk, or are you planning to strike?"

Elias stiffened. "I wish to know why she keeps me in her sights while entertaining that parade of half-wits."

Honoria took a careful step back. "Well," she said, maddeningly composed, "perhaps you should ask her."

Across the room, Florence dipped into a curtsy, her dance with Mr Layton drawing to a close. He was grinning at something she'd said, all flushed enthusiasm and eager bows, while she laughed—genuine, unhurried—and touched his arm with easy familiarity.

As she straightened and turned, her gaze caught on Elias and stopped cold.

Her eyes dropped to his cravat. A slow smile curved her

mouth. "You're wearing cream."

"I am," he replied evenly. "My valet insisted it would brighten my appearance."

She let her gaze linger a moment too long. "Well. He certainly made a choice."

Elias's jaw flexed.

She arched a brow, the picture of sweet civility. "Tell me, was it your valet's taste you were trusting, or your own?"

He extended his hand, gaze fixed to hers. "Dance with me, Miss Ashcroft."

She hesitated long enough for him to catch it. Then laid her hand in his.

He leaned in, voice dark. "Unless, of course, you're saving yourself for someone whose tailor gets more attention than his character."

They stepped onto the floor and joined the set, faces composed, but eyes locked like duellists. The early steps of the quadrille allowed his irritation to calcify into something sharper.

"You've danced with four gentlemen already," Elias said, voice low as they turned through the promenade.

"Yes," she replied.

He stiffened. "Is that… significant?"

She faltered, only slightly, but he caught it. *Good.*

He leaned in, his voice at her ear, each syllable deliberate. "You've turned the evening into a parade. Four men, all of them preening for your favour. But let's not pretend anymore."

He paused long enough to feel the way her fingers stiffened against his sleeve. "You don't want a husband," he said. "Not really." The words coiled between them like smoke.

Her chin lifted, her steps brisk and precise, though he could feel the tension rippling through her fingers.

"Oh?" she said, her voice almost pleasant, but her eyes flashed like steel. "And you presume to know my intentions?"

Her next turn around him came tighter than it should have, her skirts twisting against his thigh—a flash of wine-red satin and heat—her hand digging into his arm enough for him to feel it.

"You think because you've glimpsed a corner of my plan that you've solved me entirely?" she continued, her smile thin enough to cut.

"Tell me, Lord Blackstone—" she leaned close enough for him to feel her breath against his neck, "—does it soothe your pride to imagine that every choice I make has anything at all to do with *you*?"

"You don't want a single one of them," he said, letting the words slide between them like a blade.

Her shoulders stiffened under his hand.

"They bore you," he went on, voice quiet but merciless. "All of them. You're too clever for them, and you know it. You're not choosing a husband, you're crafting a fiction no one else is clever enough to question... except me."

He felt the faintest shiver run through her body.

"And tell *me*, Miss Ashcroft," he murmured when she returned to his reach, "how long do you intend to keep masquerading before you admit it?"

"And what," she snapped, her mask cracking enough for heat to bleed through, "do you imagine I *do* want, Lord Blackstone?"

He offered a confident, intentional smile. "Someone who argues back."

The dance pulled them apart. She spun away from him, but her eyes never left his, even when she was halfway down the line.

It was enough to make his blood spark with something perilously close to triumph. When the last note of the quadrille faded, she dropped his arm as though it burned.

He held her gaze, unflinching, and offered her a cool, ironic bow, as polite as it was mocking.

"A pleasure," he murmured, the words a dare as much as a farewell.

Before she turned, her eyes caught his, blazing with fury, pride, and something darker. And he knew, with grim satisfaction, that his words had struck true.

16

Chapter Sixteen

Florence sat rigidly on the floor of her bedchamber, sage-green skirts wrinkled beyond salvation, the once-immaculate velvet rug beneath her fingers now crushed and twisted from her grip.

Around her lay the detritus of the last evening: crumpled dance cards, smudged ink drafts of her carefully plotted list, and the shattered remains of what had once been a rather optimistic plate of lemon biscuits.

Honoria lounged nearby, perfectly composed, chin resting in her palm as she surveyed the chaos. "Shall I strike him off then? Lord Blackstone?" she asked, quill poised like a dagger.

"Immediately."

Honoria raised her brows, scratching his name out with a theatrical flourish. "A particular reason?" She ventured at last.

Florence's lips thinned. "He mocked me."

"Did he?"

"In the middle of a quadrille," she hissed. "With that ridiculous smile—at my plan. As though it were—" She broke off, the memory prickling along her skin like nettles. Her hands clenched again, nails digging into velvet. "He looked at me like he *knew*. And worse, like it *amused* him."

Honoria's expression softened, but Florence was having none of it.

"Don't say a word."

"I wasn't going to—"

"I *saw* your mouth twitch."

"I might have inhaled sharply."

"Don't." Florence reached for a biscuit and snapped it in half with far more violence than necessary, crumbs scattering across the wreckage of parchment.

"Your face is rather red."

"That's because I'm incandescent."

"With rage?"

"With *humiliation*." Florence flung the biscuit across the room. It struck the wainscoting and disintegrated. "He called it a masquerade. As though I'm—*performing*. As though protecting myself is some kind of joke." Florence groaned and flung herself back against the rug, staring at the ceiling rose like it might offer divine intervention. "I hate him."

"Yes. That much is evident." Honoria smothered a smile behind her hand, but Florence caught it anyway.

"Oh, you *like* him," she accused.

"I like what he *does* to you," Honoria replied serenely.

"He humiliates *me."*

"He rattles you." Honoria gave her a dry look. "You're rattled, Florence. It's delightful. Like watching someone try to fan themselves with the parish accounts."

"He is not a—suitor. And now I know why." Florence's voice cracked on the last word, but she covered it with a sniff.

"Shame. He was the only one who looked like he owned a

library and used it."

Honoria set the quill down and examined their battered battlefield of prospects.

Mr Stratton—wealthy, polite, and as thrilling as a damp cellar.

Mr Layton—suspiciously devoted to his dog.

Mr Redgrave—excellent lineage, far too many teeth.

Mr Farleigh—youngest son, charming, claims to read Voltaire (dubious).

Lord Blackstone—struck through several times, but still somehow legible.

"I vote we keep Mr Farleigh," Honoria said serenely. "He might be lying, but I admire the effort."

"He claimed to be fluent in Greek," Florence muttered, "and then called Homer 'that blind chap with the horse.'"

Honoria shrugged. "He's got enthusiasm."

Florence ripped the parchment from Honoria's hand and scored through Stratton's name herself.

"But he's rich!"

"And dull. I refuse to marry into ennui."

"Mr Layton?" Honoria prompted, watching her closely.

Florence hesitated. "He stays."

Honoria's brows lifted.

"He's measured," Florence admitted. "Thoughtful. He actually listened when I spoke about apprenticeship schemes. Quoted Adam Smith back to me—correctly. He listens. He even asked after the mill's weaver's union terms—*specifically*. He knew more about northern tariffs than most of our MPs."

"So… you like him?"

"I respect him," Florence said slowly. "He doesn't patronise me. He sees the business, not just the heiress behind it."

Honoria tossed up her hands. "Romantic," she muttered. "Truly, how will your heart survive it?"

Florence sighed. "That's not the point."

"So he understands numbers?"

"Yes."

"And yet, you wouldn't let him near the mill ledgers if your life depended on it."

Florence arched a brow. "Obviously not."

"Why not?"

"Because they're *mine,*" she said, simply. "He'd want to… make improvements." Her voice thinned. "And I'd murder him."

Honoria reached for the last biscuit. "Mr Redgrave?"

"Out. The teeth are unsettling," she said, dropping the parchment.

Honoria drew a decisive line through his name, then laid down the quill with an air of triumph. "Two remain."

Florence closed her eyes and pressed her palms to them, as though she could blot out the world. "The next bout?" she muttered.

Honoria's eyes gleamed with playful delight. "Mother's musicale."

Florence groaned. "Oh, not the musicale."

"Yorkshire's most eligible bachelors gathered in one stifling drawing room, while you murder a sonata at the pianoforte—anyone who stays through that deserves you."

"I *cannot* play the pianoforte."

"Precisely."

Florence cracked a smile, bleak though it was.

Honoria regarded the names one last time, then, with infuriating deliberation, tapped Blackstone's name. "He should stay," she declared.

"Absolutely not."

"Florence."

"No," she said more firmly.

Honoria held her gaze. "You've eliminated every other man for being dull, suspiciously moist, or unusually devoted to poultry. And honestly, he's the only one who looks at you like he's awake."

Florence kept her eyes on the parchment. Two names left. Two men she could manage. Men who wouldn't press or question. Men who would leave her alone.

She could control this. She could choose. So why, then, did her pulse stutter at the one name that had made her feel anything at all?

Florence's jaw tightened. She drew a thick, definitive line through Lord Blackstone's name. Then underlined the remaining two names with slow, deliberate strokes.

"There," she said coolly. "Now it's settled."

Honoria gave a brief nod, too knowing, for Florence's liking.

She turned, brushing crumbs from her skirts with more force than necessary. "I need air."

And as she strode from the room, she told herself she hadn't hesitated.

Not even for a second.

* * *

Mr Alton Webb sat draped in his mother's favourite chair, all smiles and silk waistcoat, looking as though he'd stepped straight out of a gentleman's outfitter window rather than the fields of Spain, as he claimed.

"Elias, darling," his mother gushed, her rings flashing as she gestured toward Webb, "Mr Webb served with distinction in Spain. The Wellington campaign. Isn't that marvellous?"

"Fascinating," Elias replied, not bothering to mask the edge in his voice. "I'm sure the Spanish found him equally impressive."

Mr Webb chuckled obligingly—as though Elias were joking. He wasn't.

He eyed the man coolly, a good ten years her junior. And in under ten minutes, Elias had gathered; he possessed all the substance of a polished doorknob and twice the self-importance.

Mr Webb leaned back, crossing one well-booted ankle over the other, exuding self-satisfaction.

"Hmm, yes, the Wellington campaign," he was saying to Lady Cheverley. "Madrid, Salamanca, Badajoz... dreadful business. But one learns to adapt."

Elias stood at the sideboard, a glass of brandy in hand, his eyes narrowing.

Something about the smooth way Webb said it. Too *practised*.

"You learn to adapt," Webb repeated, swirling his drink, he added almost idly, "I even crossed paths with a chap from this very county. Fellow countryman. Odd sort. Churchman now, believe it or not. But back then, quite handy with a blade." He smiled into his glass. "Strange where one's allies come from, isn't it?"

Lady Cheverley cooed, but Elias's gaze sharpened, because he knew damn well there weren't many churchmen in Yorkshire with a past like that.

He set his glass down, smoothing his sleeve. "I have business to attend to," he said, tone clipped. "And I suspect you have more tales of glory to rehearse. Do carry on."

He nodded once at his mother, once at Webb, then left, his exit polite, his disdain unmistakable.

His chamber door closed behind him with a soft thud. Elias stood there a moment, the hush of Mooredge settling in around him like mist.

Churchman now, quite handy with a blade.

Webb couldn't have meant Ward. The man was all calm sermons and garden walks," not the sort to survive Spain, let alone be sent there.

The brandy burned as he poured another and drank. Webb's words echoed, but so did the sound of his mother's laughter, light, youthful, dangerously charmed. She'd always gravitated to silver-tongued men with empty pockets and full intentions. Norbury had just been the loudest.

Webb, he suspected, was something quieter. More polished. A predator who didn't snarl, he smiled.

Well. He'd learned to read those smiles. If his mother refused to learn, Elias would do it for them both.

He sat at the desk, pulled a fresh sheet of parchment toward him, and dipped his quill without hesitation.

Dear Mr Meritt,

You are instructed to gather every available detail on one Mr Alton Webb. Former military. Now, a civilian with sudden easy fortune and suspicious affections for my mother.

If you find a wife in the attic, a debtor in the shadows, or a secret child tucked in a French convent—do let me know.

Yours with considerable impatience,

E. Blackstone

He set down the quill, sanded the ink, and folded the letter with the quiet satisfaction of a man laying the first stone of someone else's ruin.

* * *

By the next morning, Elias had determined three things: First, his mother was resplendent.

As though the last decade of her life had been nothing more than a mild inconvenience, and Webb a miraculous cure. Second, Mr Webb had far too many stories, and likely a very detailed plan that ended with his mother's fortune in his purse. And third, the only way to keep an eye on the opportunist in evening gloves was to attend every single social engagement *he* attended. Including, unfortunately, Lady Wrenthorpe's musicale.

Tom rejoiced at the news. Which was, frankly, insulting. Elias had declared that he would not be attending *any* more social gatherings this year. The announcement that he would attend the musicale had sent Tom into a frenzy of polishing, brushing, and talking far too much.

Elias was considering drowning himself in Rookhaven's duck pond.

"You'll want the mirror-bright Hessians," Tom said, bent over them, his polishing cloth moving in vigorous little circles. "And a new pair of gloves, with pearl buttons. They are more… musical."

Elias eyed him. *"Musical?"*

Tom straightened, unrepentant. "Appearance matters, my lord. People should see you and hear the violins in their heads."

Elias leaned an elbow on the mantle. "People will see me and hear wedding bells, or duelling pistols, more like."

Tom beamed at his reflection in the polished leather. "Well. That's still *something*."

The silence stretched before Tom casually added, "Will Lady Florence be there, sir?"

Elias's gaze snapped to him. "I imagine so."

Tom raised a brow, still pretending innocence. "Good. Maybe you can stare at her with that brooding death-glare while she reconsiders her suitors."

"I am *not* a suitor."

Tom smiled to himself and buffed harder. "Well," he said cheerfully, "it's a musicale. There'll be intermissions. Dark corners. Places to loiter and pretend you weren't planning any sort of encounter."

Elias didn't dignify that with a response. Instead, he drained his glass and turned toward the wardrobe.

Tom had already beaten him to it, holding up the black waistcoat with the silver stitching. It flickered in the firelight. "This one," he said. "The one that makes you look like a particularly dangerous poem."

Elias examined the waistcoat. And to his quiet horror, he didn't disagree.

17

Chapter Seventeen

The Wrenthorpe drawing-room had been repurposed as a war room.

Not in name, but the glint in Honoria's eye and the steep angle of Florence's chin left little doubt.

"Right," Honoria declared, unfurling the evening's printed programme across a damask footstool like a general plotting siege. "You have six hours before the finale, a finite supply of punch, and at least a dozen mamas with unwed sons watching like duchesses guarding a bloodline. We must be voracious."

Florence folded her arms. "You're taking this very seriously."

Honoria shot her a look so withering that a passing footman winced, nearly sloshing the punch. "Florence. Please. There will be matrons in this room who have trained for years to sniff out a weak suitor and sink them before the first aria. If we don't control the battlefield, we lose."

"Fine," she said. "But I am not smiling at anyone with a mother in the room. That's where I draw the line."

"You're choosing a husband," Honoria said, flipping the programme like a croupier with cards. "Or in your case, a decorative shield. How do you want to narrow the shortlist?"

Florence smirked despite herself. "Fine. Let's split the evening into halves."

"First half, Mr Theodore Farleigh."

Florence tilted her head thoughtfully. "Middling intelligence. Tolerably polite. Cheekbones carrying the rest."

"Also," Honoria added, tapping her fan, "not repulsed by women who work. His exact words were: 'If it keeps them busy, I suppose it's fine.'"

Florence gave a dry smile. "A glowing endorsement. Nothing like a man who tolerates you."

"Second half, Mr Henry Layton."

Florence hesitated. "He brought me a book last week. *Practical Treatises on Modern Weaving Techniques.* With notes in the margins." Florence's mouth twitched. "He's… not unpleasant. Predictable, but thoughtful. Like a well-made coat."

Honoria leaned closer. "A coat?"

"A reliable one," Florence said primly.

"His income," Honoria countered, "could fund a modest war. You could test steam engines in his drawing room."

Florence sighed. "Fine. By then, I'll be half-drunk on elderflower wine and less likely to care."

"And Lord Blackstone…"

Florence narrowed her eyes. "Irrelevant."

"Oh, of course," Honoria murmured, voice all syrup and daggers. Her fan snapped shut with a decisive *click*. "Because Lord Blackstone will obviously behave himself and stay in the shadows where you left him."

Honoria stared at her, "he's still attending tonight. And I daresay he'll be wearing one of those terribly distracting waistcoats you keep *not* noticing."

"Let him," Florence said, smoothing her skirts with unnecessary precision. "He can lurk near the punch bowl and smoulder at someone else."

"Florence," Honoria said lightly, "he only ever smoulders at *you*."

Florence said nothing. But her fingers kept smoothing that same patch of fabric long after it lay flat.

* * *

Guests were assembled on satin-upholstered chairs and velvet-backed settees, their expressions eager, like foxhounds pretending to enjoy the hunt for culture rather than iniquity.

Honoria settled herself at the pianoforte, her gown shimmering in shades of lilac and frost. The room was hushed and expectant.

Elias entered like a downpour—all broad shoulders, storm-dark eyes, and an expression carved from stone. Beside him, Lady Cheverley sparkled with amethysts and ambition, like a woman who'd spent the past week either falling in love or planning an ambush.

He barely registered the bowing footman or murmured greetings. His attention, he assured himself, was fixed on two matters, neither of which, by any rational measure, had anything to do with Florence Ashcroft.

First, his mother's mysterious suitor sat across the room in an obscenely well-cut tail coat and looked far too pleased for a man who'd wandered into enemy territory.

And second... *well.* His eyes betrayed him. Across the room, in pale blue silk, Florence Ashcroft had taken her seat beside Honoria. She took her seat like he wasn't even in the room.

Which irritated him more than he'd admit. Even to himself. He adjusted the cuffs of his black coat with unnecessary precision. "I'm not here for her," he muttered.

His mother turned with a faint smile. "Did you say something, darling?"

"Not at all," he replied through clenched teeth, his eyes still fixed on Florence.

Lady Cheverley leaned in. "Now, do behave," she murmured. "I'd prefer you didn't frighten Mr Webb before I've properly decided whether I enjoy his company."

Elias's gaze flicked back to the gentleman in question, all laughter and overconfidence.

"And don't scowl," his mother added, sweetly.

"I only scowl," Elias said, with a cool smile. "When provoked."

Honoria began to play. For the first few bars, her fingers fluttered like butterflies over the ivory keys, hesitant but recognisable, the melody sweet enough to draw polite nods from the audience. It didn't last; her confidence faltered, and notes clashed. A sharp dissonance made one of the matrons in the front row flinch.

With a rigid spine and an unwavering smile, Honoria continued through the passage. Florence leaned discreetly toward her, murmured something, and pointed at the music. Honoria nodded tightly, corrected herself, and coaxed out a few passable bars, but the damage was done.

The last few notes stumbled to a halt like a carriage losing a wheel, and the applause, though polite, was mercifully brief.

Elias hadn't clapped.

Because Florence, bent at Honoria's side, lit by the amber

glow of the chandeliers, snatched his gaze entirely, and against his will. There was a brightness to her, beauty in the chaos, like someone who thrived under scrutiny.

She looked content, *he thought.* As though society were another game, she intended to win while everyone else played by the rules.

This was going to be a very long evening.

Florence rose, dipping a graceful curtsy. Honoria beamed, ever the optimist, and flitted toward the punch table, likely in search of something strong enough to rinse the shame of her performance from memory.

A gentleman approached Florence. Jacket stiff with starch. Chin so slight it was theoretical.

Elias's lips pressed into a line that dared interruption.

"Mr Webb seems in good spirits," his mother murmured, smoothing her skirts as she bestowed a warm, lingering smile across the room.

Elias followed her gaze.

Gleaming boots, glib eyes. Smiling like she'd proposed and he'd graciously accepted.

He stood near the hearth, head tipped toward Mrs Fairfax, who laughed behind her fan like a schoolgirl, cheeks pink with approval.

"I told you." His mother leaned in, voice pleased. "He's been very good to the Rookhaven Development Committee. Offered to underwrite the cost of new roofs for the almshouses."

Elias arched a brow. "Charity? Or investment?"

"Must you greet every kindness like it hides a blade?" she said with a little sigh.

He leaned closer. "You do realise he oils his sideburns."

She patted his arm as though he were a tiresome spaniel. "So did your father."

"Yes," Elias said, "and look where that got him."

With a dismissive tsk, Lady Cheverley swept toward Webb, her silks catching the light as she moved, leaving the rest of the room in her perfumed wake.

Elias stayed where he was, watching the interplay. The doting smiles. The murmured praise. The nods of approval that Webb collected like coins.

His expression darkened by degrees. Let the gentry fawn, his mother flirt, and the fiend smile until his teeth cracked. Elias would wait for his agent's report. And he would deal with the Webb problem, with facts, questions, and calibrated disdain.

He crossed the floor, cutting through gowns and gossip, not slowing for pleasantries. Honoria stood near the edge, her gaze fixed on the crowd, her fan still against her hand, the very picture of polite curiosity and mild contempt.

At her elbow stood a gentleman mid-sheep monologue, braying on about blue ribbons and bloodlines. Elias didn't catch the beginning—nor, mercifully, the end—but suspected neither held much promise.

She endured him with the composure of a woman debating whether to stab herself with her own hairpin.

"Miss Wrenthorpe," Elias murmured, executing a slight bow. "A quiet word."

Honoria turned to him at once, her smile determined, like someone grasping at an escape. "Lord Blackstone," she said, a little too grandly to be sincere. "You survived the performance, then?"

"Barely," he replied, his gaze following the sheep enthusiast as he melted back into the crowd.

Honoria laughed. "Florence," she confided, tilting her head

toward the pianoforte, "is an excellent rider. She is not a musician."

"Yes," Elias said. "I'd gathered."

He angled his head toward Florence. "Tell me," he murmured, voice low, "Is he at the top of her shortlist?"

Honoria took her time. She sipped from her punch, eyes glittering. "Indeed."

Elias's mouth curved into something that wasn't quite a smile. "He looks," he said, watching the man preen, "like he's never said no to a mirror."

"You're jealous," Honoria said sweetly, though the weight behind the words was anything but.

"I'm observant," Elias said coldly. "Miss Ashcroft is clever enough to see through him."

Honoria's eyes sparkled with wicked amusement. "She sees a man who won't interfere. No fuss. That's the point."

She cast a glance around the room, "You may not be on the shortlist. But you're not *forgotten* either."

Elias narrowed his eyes. "And what, precisely, do you propose I do?"

Honoria's fan snapped shut with a satisfying click. "If you wish to see her shackled to Mr Damp-Napkin over there, the bore with opinions on curtain tassels, by all means, do nothing."

He set his jaw.

"Or," she added, voice silk over steel, "you might consider clearing the field."

Elias arched a brow. "You're suggesting sabotage."

"I'm suggesting," she said, arch and unapologetic, "that the lady is not as immune to you as she pretends. The rest… is simply strategy."

He looked back toward Florence. She was tilting her head,

lips quirking—amused, or on the brink of abandoning all civility. It was difficult to tell. Her suitor, oblivious, was gesturing with a champagne flute and sloshing droplets onto her sleeve.

"Oh dear," Honoria murmured, far too pleased. "He's making her cross."

"She doesn't suffer fools," Elias said, eyes fixed on the scene.

"She doesn't suffer anyone," Honoria replied lightly. "Except you. You, Lord Blackstone, she takes the time to argue with you."

"She argues with everyone."

"No," Honoria said, leaning in. "She dismantles others. She *debates* you."

Elias said nothing.

"I suppose you'll be *disrupting* the evening," she went on, as casually as one might comment on the weather.

"I said no such thing."

Her smile suggested she hadn't believed a word. "Shall I tell you his name?"

Elias folded his arms. "Go on."

"Mr Farleigh," Honoria murmured, her eyes skimming the ballroom. "Recently inherited a sizeable estate, fond of poetry, pigeons, and very much enamoured with the idea of a quiet life by a roaring fire, with a wife who never raises her voice."

Farleigh was now reading from a folded scrap of paper, his expression rapt. Florence looked as though she might chew through the pianoforte rather than endure another stanza.

"She's building an empire. He's waiting for applause when he enters a room," Elias said flatly.

"Mmm," Honoria agreed, sipping her punch. "What will you do?"

His eyes didn't leave Florence. Her expression hovered between forced courtesy and outright revolt.

"I'll... discourage him."

"How?"

"I've not yet decided."

Her fan flicked open with a snap. "Do try to keep it *lawful*."

Elias didn't return her smile.

18

Chapter Eighteen

It was a white lie.

Hardly more than a passing comment. Nothing cruel.

"She's allergic," Elias said, voice like warm honey. "Pigeons. Breaks out in a rash. Can't breathe. It's all very *delicate*." He let the word hang. "I've seen less dramatic fainting spells at Vauxhall."

Mr Farleigh—looking appropriately stricken—went a shade paler. "Pigeons?"

"Indeed."

Farleigh blinked, lips parting in horror.

Elias took a delicate sip of his brandy, letting the silence stretch.

A moment later, Farleigh leaned toward his mother, whispering fast and low. Her eyes widened. She clutched her pearls.

Two seconds after that, Mrs Farleigh was tugging the elbow of Mrs Fairfax, who gasped and covered her mouth with her fan like she'd witnessed a public duel.

Within minutes, the whisper passed from one velvet-clad matron to another, fuelled by concern, confusion, and the quiet satisfaction of being the first to know something someone else didn't. The word was out. Florence Ashcroft, darling of the Wrenthorpe musicale, had a *tragic sensitivity to pigeons*.

Farleigh fled. And Florence? Florence heard.

Elias stood by a window, the picture of idle satisfaction. Smug didn't quite cover it.

She marched across the room, wine glass clutched like a weapon, and hissed through her teeth, "You blackguard."

He blinked, all innocence. "I beg your pardon?"

"You heard me."

She didn't wait for a reply; she spun on her heel and strode off into the hall. Naturally, he followed into quieter shadow. Moonlight pooled between the velvet-draped windows of a side passage when she whirled on him, eyes blazing.

"Pigeons?"

He gave a mild shrug. "Ah."

She stepped closer, fire in her voice. "Are you *daft*?"

"A touch."

"You told Mr Farleigh I was allergic to pigeons."

"It's a common allergy."

"It's a *lie*."

"You looked nauseous when he—"

"And now," she snapped, cutting him off, "my entire plan is in tatters."

He had the audacity to look *pleased*.

"You're smiling. Stop smiling."

"I'm not smiling."

"You are."

He pressed his lips into a thin line, but the gleam in his eyes betrayed him. "I thought you'd be grateful."

"Grateful," she echoed.

"He was reading you poetry. About *pigeons*."

"I *like* poetry."

"You looked like you wanted to leap from an upstairs window."

"That's beside the point!" She jabbed a finger into his chest, hard enough that he glanced down in faint surprise.

"Why do you care who I marry?"

"I don't."

"Liar."

His gaze flicked to her hand, still resting against his chest.

"Your interference is unacceptable," she hissed.

"I'm not trying to ruin it."

"Then what are you trying to do?"

His eyes darkened, voice low. "I'm trying to understand whether I'm the flaw in your plan… or something you're too afraid to name."

The passage pressed in around them. Her closeness flooded his senses, the warmth of her skin, the faint tremor in her fingers, the way her gaze dropped for half a second to his mouth.

"I should slap you," she said, her voice barely above a whisper.

"You should," he murmured, but he didn't move away.

Their eyes locked. The air between them pulled taut as a wire. One more breath, one more inch, and—

"Florence?" came Honoria's bright call from the ballroom, slicing through the moment like cold steel.

Florence jerked back. Her chest rose and fell rapidly, her eyes fierce.

"We are not finished," she snapped. Then turned, skirts flaring, leaving only velvet shadows and the echo of what could have been.

* * *

It had been three days since the musicale. Since Elias Blackstone had looked her in the eye and asked if he was something she was afraid of.

Florence had thought of little else since. And so, with as much sense as she could summon, she had decided she would marry Mr Layton. He was the safest choice. Judicious and steady. A man unlikely to interfere with her life, or set it alight.

To that end, she had arranged a small dinner for Mr Layton, herself and her father. Nothing elaborate. A calm, reasonable evening in which she might begin the business of securing her future.

Only the parlour was too warm. Or perhaps it was simply Florence, sitting far too still beside her father, trying not to betray the storm coiling in her stomach.

Because across the table—not Mr Layton, not safety, not sense—sat Elias Blackstone. Looking like sin dressed in brushed navy wool, and if he aimed to provoke, he was halfway there. In Yorkshire, that smug expression got people shoved in rivers.

Her father was utterly charmed. Laughing, even. Hanging on Elias's every word as though he'd never heard such wit over roast beef.

Florence twisted her napkin in her lap, her smile a brittle thing held together by sheer force of will. She should have known he'd ruin it.

Mr Layton had sent a note—late, rushed, full of vague apologies about a family urgency. A weak excuse. One she didn't believe for a second.

And now here *he* was—knife in one hand, wineglass in the other—seated where Layton was meant to be. He'd even brought a bottle of wine from a well-known London merchant, known for supplying dukes and diplomats. How *thoughtful.*

Her father beamed. "Very fine wine, Lord Blackstone," he wheezed, eyes bright. "You'll make Yorkshire more refined yet."

Elias bowed his head with maddening composure. "I shall try, sir. Though I daresay it's Yorkshire that may yet refine me."

Florence made a strangled noise in the back of her throat. "We can but hope," she muttered, her hand flattening against the table with barely restrained force.

Elias raised his wine in her direction. A silent toast.

Florence very nearly threw hers at his infuriatingly pleased, aristocratic head.

After dinner, her father excused himself, promising to return after his tonic. The moment his footsteps faded, Florence rose from her chair with the grace of a queen and the fury of a woman scorned. "You arrogant, interfering—."

Elias looked up, maddeningly calm. "Good evening to you, too, Miss Ashcroft. Always a pleasure to feel so... warmly received."

"Don't pretend with me. Don't sit there as though you haven't humiliated me in my own home."

He didn't flinch. "I thought I was saving you the effort of pretending Layton was *enough.*"

"What effort?" She hissed. "You mean choosing the one man who fits every requirement? The one I'd already decided to marry—until you ruined it?

He leaned forward, voice low. "You're angry because I turned up instead of that charming little bore you chose as your future?"

"Yes," she snapped. "You had *no right*. No place at that table."

He set his glass down. When he spoke, the polish dropped. And what remained was steel. "I'll tell you what right I've got, Miss Ashcroft. The same right any man at this table might claim. Only I won't sit by while you throw yourself at the first man polite enough not to contradict you. Layton wouldn't have lasted a season."

Her spine stiffened. "You presume a great deal."

"I see a great deal."

He stood, and the space between them contracted.

She lifted her chin, defiant, but her pulse betrayed her,thudding against the base of her throat.

"You speak to men," he said, voice pitched low, "like you've been managing them your entire life."

He stopped just short of her. The scent of fire and something sharper clung to him. "But me?"

His gaze held hers. "You look at me like I might be the first who could actually *keep up*."

Something coiled in her chest.

"So what is it you're afraid of, Miss Ashcroft? Because it isn't me. And it isn't marriage."

He held the silence long enough to sting.

"Why do you still think you have to face the world alone?"

She glared at him, fury and panic twisting in her ribs. "That's irrelevant."

"Not to me."

"You are not part of my plan," she said, quieter now, but still fierce.

"No," he said. "But I could be. If you stopped running."

"Running?" The word exploded out of her, in disbelief.

He stepped in closer, and the air shifted with him. His voice dropped, solid as oak. "You want a husband in name only. A ghost in the house. A man who vanishes into the background." His tone was resolute. "I won't give you that."

"Good," she bit out, chin high. "Because I'm not offering you the chance."

At that, he smiled. That insufferable victorious smile, that made her want to slap him, or drag him bodily into the nearest cupboard.

"We'll see."

And without another word, Elias Blackstone turned and strode from the room.

She watched him leave, like a man who *knew* he'd unravelled every last nerve in her body.

Florence exhaled. She turned to pour herself another glass of wine, cursing under her breath when the stem slipped in her trembling fingers.

Footsteps broke the silence behind her. Her father?

No.

Elias Blackstone stepped back into the room.

Unbridled fury surged. "Oh, what is it now?" she snapped. "Come back to—"

She didn't finish. Because he was already there. He crossed the room in three long strides—a storm unbottled—and kissed her. It wasn't tentative, but defiant.

One hand curved around her neck, fingers firm, tilting her to him like he'd been waiting for this since the day they met. The other braced hard on the table behind her, boxing her in, steadying himself, as though the sheer force of it might knock him to his knees.

It was every argument they'd ever had. Every glare, every maddening breath. Every impossible, tangled thing she'd felt about him—poured into a single, devastating kiss.

Florence broke. Her fingers clutched his lapels, desperate and anchoring. She gasped against his mouth, and still, still she kissed him back. Fiercely. Like sense had left the room, and she wanted nothing of it back.

When he pulled away enough to see her, his breath was ragged. His eyes, dark and dazed, flicked over her. Like he couldn't quite believe he'd done it.

Florence stood frozen. Her heart lodged somewhere between her chest and his hand, still hovering at her neck.

He exhaled, voice raw. "I didn't plan to do that."

She blinked. "Clearly."

"I was halfway to the door."

"I noticed." The silence was heavy and bruising. "Why did you come back?"

Elias studied her, like she was something fragile—something he feared he'd never be allowed to touch again. The intensity of it set her on edge.

"Because you drive me mad," he said. "You make plans with meticulous patience, and yet you lose your temper with me like a hailstorm. And I can't stop wondering…" He exhaled, gaze steady. "What your life would look like if you weren't trying to control every inch."

He leaned in, lips brushing hers without contact, purely breath and promise. "Because I'd rather kiss you than walk away and let you believe no one sees you."

Florence swallowed hard. That was inconveniently swoon-worthy.

And unacceptable. She pushed back enough to breathe, to

remember herself. The armour slid into place like a well-worn cloak. "This changes nothing, Lord Blackstone."

He smiled then, the smile of a man who knew he was already inside the walls. "Oh," he murmured, turning toward the door, "I sincerely hope not."

This time, when Elias Blackstone walked away, he didn't even look back.

19

Chapter Nineteen

Mooredge was still when Elias returned, still enough that his footsteps struck the stone like judgment. From the east parlour came his mother's laughter, warm and unguarded. He slowed.

A smooth, confident drawl followed, curling down the hallway. Familiar. Far too familiar. Webb.

Elias's hand flexed at his side. For a moment, he turned toward the sound, ready to stride in, rip it to shreds, and damn the consequences.

He pivoted, not tonight. Climbing the stairs two at a time, he shut himself in his chamber with a force that rattled the doorframe.

Tom looked up from the armchair by the hearth, book open, brow furrowed in scholarly concentration.

"Evening, sir," he said brightly. "I'm reading about the Napoleon knot. Very dashing. Not at all like the lavender disaster last week—"

"Tom," Elias cut in, already shrugging off his coat and pitching it across the bed. "Do me a kindness and don't speak to me about neckwear. Or anything… continental."

Tom blinked, wounded. "Understood, sir."

Elias ran a hand through his hair and began pacing, brusque and agitated, like a man in a cell awaiting sentence.

Tom watched him before shutting his book. "If it's not my place to say, sir, forgive me," he ventured, "but… is something the matter?"

Elias fixed him with a look so bleak it could've cracked stone. "Tom," he asked, "have you ever courted a woman?"

Tom's eyebrows flew up. "Oh. Well. Not exactly, sir. But I did once spend an entire village fete buying lavender soap from Miss Parker, hoping she might look up from her ribbons and notice me."

Elias stared.

Tom cleared his throat. "Didn't work, sir. She married the butcher's lad."

Elias pinched the bridge of his nose. "Excellent. My valet reads about French neckwear and pines after soap girls, and *this* is who I'm taking advice from."

Tom sat up, brightening. "I make an excellent confidant, sir. The book says so. *Chapter Seven: Maintaining Masterly Confidence Through Discreet Counsel.*"

Elias sighed and resumed pacing. "I'm doomed."

Tom forged ahead. "My sister Mary. Married a carpenter. Courted her for a year. Brought her sweetmeats, beeswax candles, even a chicken."

"A chicken."

"A live one," Tom confirmed, still delighted by the memory. "Our Mary was very impressed."

Elias stared harder.

Tom coughed. "I wouldn't recommend that for Lady Florence."

"No," Elias muttered. "No chickens."

Tom shifted, still clutching his book. "If I may… what Mary liked best wasn't the chicken. It was that he noticed things. How her knee ached in winter. That she hated draughts. Her favourite kind of pie."

Elias shook his head. "Are you suggesting I win Lady Florence's hand with pie?"

Tom straightened, hopeful. "If you knew which one was her favourite, sir."

Elias laughed and sank into the chair by the fire. One arm draped over the backrest as he watched the flames dance. "She likes order," he murmured. "Control. Purpose. She's planning her marriage like a military campaign."

Tom nodded sagely. "Then be the disorder, sir."

Elias's head snapped up. "What?"

Tom shrugged, half-sheepish, half-defiant. "If the others are predictable, maybe you're the one who isn't. Show her you see her. Not the mill. Not the marriage plan. *Her*."

The fire crackled between them. "You might be an actual genius, Tom."

Tom flushed to his ears. "Thank you, sir."

Then, hopefully— "Shall I practise the Napoleon knot? Just in case?"

Elias groaned and dropped his head into his hands.

Tom beamed. "Very good, sir. No knots."

* * *

Rookhaven market sprawled across the square in a riot of

barrels and wagons, thick with the scent of hay, wet sheep, and too many people talking over one another. Dogs weaved between boots. A butcher argued with a baker, and a barrow of pears tipped sideways, vanishing into the road.

Elias pushed through the crowd with grim purpose. He paused at a flower stall, blooms bursting in wild, unruly bundles.

None of them suited her. The Michaelmas daisies? Too timid. The pale pink roses? She'd loathe them.

A battered tin bucket caught his eye, camellias, of all things. Rare for Yorkshire. Costly, too. Their unapologetic bloom carried a certain defiance, all controlled beauty and unyielding grace. He bought an armful.

At the confectioners, he dallied longer than he cared to, staring at neat rows of ribboned boxes while people behind him sighed impatiently.

Sugared hearts? Too saccharine. Honeycomb? Childish. Dark chocolate spiced truffles—exceptionally refined, unpredictable, very Florence. He paid and turned to leave.

A girl, no more than ten, sat by the pond, her hem soaked, clutching a bent bonnet in her lap and blinking fast. A basket of potatoes spilled at her feet.

Her mother's voice rose from across the green, blunt and tired: *"Annie! For the love of God, I told you not to drop that—"*

Elias crouched. Collected the potatoes and pressed a silver coin into the girl's palm.

"Buy her something," he said. "Say it's from you."

The girl blinked. "Lord Blackstone?"

He straightened. "Don't tell anyone."

She grinned, gap-toothed. "I won't."

He turned on his heel and strode back to his horse, flowers in

one hand, chocolates under
his arm—like a man preparing for either courtship or combat.

* * *

Florence met him in the hall. Or rather, stormed into it with a ledger in hand, a pencil behind her ear, and the air of a woman fully prepared to flay a man alive using only numbers and fury.

"I've brought you a gift," Elias said, flowers in hand, voice measured, like a man determined to do things properly, even if it killed him.

Florence eyed the bouquet as though it might bite. She took them, suspicion in every line of her posture.

"Camellias?"

"They reminded me of you." He handed her the box.

Her eyes narrowed. "Ah. Bribery?"

"Flattery," he said. "If it were bribery, there'd be contracts involved."

She opened the lid, plucked out a truffle, and bit down. "... Revolting. I detest chocolate."

"No one detests chocolate," he said, aggrieved.

Florence smirked, but she didn't hand the box back.

"Unfathomable woman," he muttered under his breath.

"But..." She glanced down at the camellias. "The flowers are fine."

Not praise, but not dismissal, either. "Would you ride with me?" he asked, voice even, threaded with enough gravity to make it feel like more than a whim.

"No."

His scowl came instantly.

"It wouldn't be proper," she added, with maddening calm. "I ride only with my intended."

Elias paused. "I might become such a man."

Her eyes snapped to his. "No, my lord. You could not."

He didn't laugh. Didn't sneer. He stood there, assessing her with enduring patience. "And why not?"

Florence's fingers tightened around the stems. "Because I value peace. And you..." Her chin lifted. "You are the very opposite of it."

He inclined his head, the motion slow. "As you say."

She watched him, wariness flickering behind her composure, as though she feared he might force the matter.

But he didn't. His voice lowered. "I didn't come to press you," he said. "Or chase you into some corner where you'd feel forced to yield. That would suit neither of us."

He glanced once, pointedly, at the flowers in her grip. "I came to court you. If you'll allow it. No sabotage. No tricks."

Still, she said nothing. But she hadn't thrown the chocolates at his head. That counted for something.

Elias let a breath go through his nose. "I mean only to remain. Until you stop seeing me as a threat and start seeing me as a man who knows you. And would never ask you to change."

The silence was deafening. So he stepped back, putting distance between them with measured grace.

At the threshold, he paused. "I should warn you," he said, voice velvet-wrapped and dangerous, "those chocolates are cursed."

Her gaze snapped up. "Cursed?"

He nodded, solemn. "Anyone foolish enough to eat two is doomed to fall hopelessly in love with me."

She scoffed. "A feeble enchantment."

"They've yet to fail," he said, bowing low.

And then he was gone.

He had given her space.

And she had kept the flowers.

* * *

Florence stood at her bedroom window, watching the sun slip behind the trees, her brow furrowed. She should have thrown the chocolates out. Or fed them to the goats. But here they were. Unapologetic and stubbornly delicious.

"You said they were revolting," Honoria remarked, lifting the nearly empty box from the dressing table.

"I stand by it," Florence replied primly.

Honoria held one between two fingers. "You ate seven."

"I was confirming they were all equally unpleasant."

"Oh yes, very diligent," Honoria said, flopping back onto the bed with a grin. "So. When do you plan to make him your betrothed?"

"Never."

The word hung too long in the air. Honoria sat up, the amusement fading from her face. "But he's lodged himself in your thoughts."

Florence sighed. "I know."

"Then what in heaven's name—?"

"I can't, Honoria."

"Why?"

Florence turned from the window, voice calm. "Because he kissed me," she said, picking a camelia from the vase. "And I liked it."

Honoria gave a soft, bewildered laugh. "Well, that's rather the point—"

Florence cut her off. "And if I married him… if I touched him…" Her voice wavered. "I wouldn't stop. I wouldn't want to stop."

Honoria stilled.

"And that," Florence went on, eyes hard, "leads to children. And I don't want children."

Shock flickered across Honoria's face.

"I was the death of my mother."

Florence's words landed like iron. Honoria froze.

"She died giving me life," Florence continued, voice flat. "And it broke my father. He never looked the same again, not according to the maids. He's still not—I will not do that to someone else. I will not risk dying, to—" She stopped herself. Breathed. When she spoke again, it was with a fury that had waited years.

"I can't."

Honoria rose from the bed, crossing the room. "You told me once about your mother," she breathed. "I just thought…"

"What?" Florence asked, voice cracking. "That I'd change my mind? That a kiss from a brooding lord would undo years of knowing what marriage costs women?"

Honoria hesitated. Whispering almost to herself, "I thought maybe he would be different."

Florence's lips smoothed into something too tired to be a smile. "He *is* different, that's the problem." Her fingers tightened around the camelia in her hand until the stem snapped.

She let it fall. "I could love him, Honoria."

Honoria's face crumpled into something soft and shining. "Then let him in."

Florence shook her head, her chin trembling. "I can't. If I love him, I might let go."

Her eyes fell to the dressing table, to the cursed chocolates.

"And if I do…" Her voice broke. "I could lose everything."

Honoria reached for her then, drawing her into a quiet embrace. And for the first time in years, Florence let herself feel it.

20

Chapter Twenty

The morning air bit mercilessly against Elias's cheeks as he crossed the rear grounds. The moors beyond glimmered with frost, and a flock of sheep muttered to themselves on the hillside.

Calder was waiting by the wall that marked the orchard's edge, cap in hand, a bundle of plans tucked under one arm.

"Morning, m'lord," he said, his words were rough as ever, but almost proud in the way he gestured to the orchard.

Elias folded his arms, gaze narrowing on the land beyond. "Well?" he said.

Calder grinned. "The orchard's halfway cleared. Trees'll go in come spring. Sheep are settled in the east field. Fencing's near done—got some lads from Rookhaven to help lay it proper. Kitchen gardens started too. Maud's already had her pick of cabbages and carrots, and demanded more planting. You'd think she was the overseer.

"Hmm. Sounds like progress," said Elias.

"Aye," Calder said. "Bit of hard work and Yorkshire bloody-mindedness, and there'll be summat to be proud of again. Even got the mason coming back next week to look at the drainage stone."

Elias glanced back toward the house. "Good, you know where to find me should your purse strings tighten."

Calder chuckled and tipped his cap. "Aye, m'lord. Good to have a Blackstone around what gives a damn."

The clatter of hooves on gravel drew their attention. The mail coach rattled to a halt. A footman hurried to collect a stack of letters.

"Expecting anything?" Calder asked, squinting.

"Always," Elias murmured.

The footman approached, breathless, and handed the stack over with a polite bow. "This one's marked urgent, m'lord. From London."

Elias's fingers closed around the letter. The handwriting—neat, precise, unimpressed with flourish—was unmistakable. Mr Merrit.

He tucked the rest of the letters under his arm and opened Merrit's with his thumb right there on the path. The report was as efficient as the man himself:

> *Webb served as a quartermaster in Spain but was dismissed under suspicion of irregular dealings. Since returning, he has made a career of charming lonely widows and extracting money under various pretexts—investment schemes, fictitious debts. He has no title, no inheritance, and two outstanding warrants (Portsmouth & London). Recommend you intervene before he makes himself indispensable to Lady Cheverley.*

He folded the letter and slipped it into his pocket. "Thank you,

Merrit," he murmured to himself. He turned on his heel and strode back to the Hall. Time to cut the snake from the garden.

The clock on the mantel ticked with maddening precision as Elias sat in the drawing room, the fire casting gloomy shadows against the stone. He'd been sitting half an hour already, his mother's laughter drifting from the floor above. She was humming. Humming, for God's sake.

The door opened without announcement. Lady Cheverley swept in, a vision of plum silk and confidence. She halted when she saw him, one leg crossed, his hands steepled against his chin.

"Well," she drawled. "You look like a man about to throw himself on his sword. Please don't bleed on the rug."

Elias didn't rise. "You've been very busy," he said.

"Not nearly busy enough. Yorkshire is dreadfully dull."

"Is that what you call it? Dull?"

She tilted her head, amused. "What would you call it?"

"Lonely," he said flatly.

Her smile faltered. "Careful, Elias. You're beginning to sound like your father."

He leaned back in the chair. "No. Father never took notice, did he? Too consumed with his name and his mistresses to see his wife scraping happiness out of gossip and wine."

Her spine stiffened, but her smile remained.

"I know what you've been chasing," Elias said, his voice dropping. "In London. Here. Webb doesn't differ from the others. A trinket to wear until he tarnishes. But tell me, mother—" his eyes bored into her like steel—"have you ever *been* happy?"

The silence that followed was blistering.

When she spoke, her voice was softer. "You presume much."

"I'm your son. I don't presume; I know."

Before she could retort, carriage wheels cut through gravel. A moment later, the butler's voice called: "Mr Alton Webb, my lady."

Lady Cheverley's expression brightened, like nothing had passed between them. "Ah," she purred, smoothing a hand over her skirts. "Perfect timing."

Elias rose, and he turned as Webb entered with effortless charm.

"Good evening, my lady. Lord Blackstone," Webb said with a wide grin.

"Mr Webb. Do come in. We have unfinished business," said Elias coldly.

Webb faltered but pressed on. "Oh?" he chuckled, though the sound rang false. "Business before pleasure, is it?"

Elias reached into his coat and unfolded the letter from Merrit with deliberate care.

"It seems you've been very busy. Quartermaster in Spain—dismissed for irregular dealings. And since? You've charmed widows, draining them with fabricated debts and fraudulent investments. There are warrants in Portsmouth and London. You're a leech, Webb. And you've found my mother *very* accommodating."

Lady Cheverley's head snapped toward him. "Elias!" Her voice cut through the air. "How dare you? How dare you speak to him—to me—like this? Flinging wild accusations with no proof—"

Elias turned to her, eyes glinting. "Mother," he said sharply. "You know me. I don't speak unless I already have the proof. This—" he held up the letter and let it drop to the table "—is only the polite version."

Webb stepped forward, face tightening. "This is absurd. Fabrications. I've enemies from Spain. Competitors. I'm no stranger to slander—"

"You're no stranger to debt and fraud, either," Elias cut in.

Webb's smoothness cracked. "You *and* your father from what she's told me…," he sneered, his voice ugly now. "Both arrogant. Blind to what your mother wanted. But I see her. I give her what she needs. She deserves more than your suffocating 'protection.'"

Lady Cheverley gasped—at Webb's words or his tone, Elias couldn't tell.

Elias stepped closer until the air between them was heavy and charged. "You're right about one thing," he said dangerously. "She deserves more. More than scraps. More than liars like you. I fought a duel once for her honour, Webb. Don't think for a moment I wouldn't do it again."

He took another step. Webb stepped back. "Leave Yorkshire," Elias went on, voice lethal. "Tonight—or by morning, the magistrate will have you in irons. And if he doesn't get to you, I will."

Webb's mask fell away. His mouth gaped as he spat: "You self-righteous bastard. I pity Miss Ashcroft. You think she wants your kind of love? Cold and lonely?"

The poisonous words hung there, but Elias barely heard them. He was already moving. One more step and he could see the vein pulsing in Webb's throat, smell the sour tang of fear on him. His fingers itched. His blood sang with the familiar heat. There had been a time not so long ago when he wouldn't have stopped. When he would've drawn steel, raised his fist or sent a bullet through that smirk without hesitation. But something steadied him. *Someone.* He forced a breath out through his teeth, reigning himself back by inches. His hand flexed once at his side.

Elias opened his mouth. “Go—”

Webb turned on his heel and stalked out. The door thudded shut behind him.

Lady Cheverley didn’t look at Elias for a long, brittle moment. Her lip trembled, though she hid it with a bitter smile. “I suppose I’ve been a fool.”

“No,” he said, surprising them both. “Just lonely.”

She smiled, small, broken, but honest at last. “Thank you, darling,” she breathed. “For seeing what I wouldn’t.”

He moved a step closer, his voice gentler than before. “I’ve always watched you,” he said. “You’ve collected everything—jewels, gossip, men, stories—everything but what you wanted. Even you don’t seem to know what that is.”

Her breath caught, though she tried to cover it with a scoff. “You do not know what it’s like to… to need someone. To hope they see you and…” she swallowed hard. “But perhaps you will soon enough.”

His mouth ticked. “Perhaps.”

She smoothed her skirts. “You’ll marry your Miss Ashcroft. And you’ll want me out of your way, of course. A wife needs her space, and you’ve almost rebuilt Mooredge now. You don’t want me poking about and scandalising the neighbours.”

“That isn’t what I want,” Elias said.

“What *do* you want, darling?”

He hesitated before he answered honestly. “For you to be happy.”

That seemed to take her by surprise. Her eyes met his, wet, and proud all at once—and she laughed, soft and rueful. “You make it sound so simple.”

"It could be."

She considered him and looked back at the fire. "Perhaps I shall return to London again. After you're settled. You and Miss Ashcroft will have better things to do than worry about me. And someone should live in the London house, after all."

Elias folded his arms, brow furrowed, as he thought of Florence—of how readily he'd take up his place at Ashcroft Manor if that's what she wanted, how he'd let Mooredge go to ruin again if it meant waking up under her roof. Whatever bargain she asked of him, he'd do it. But separate roofs? Never.

His mother smiled. "And perhaps…" she added, a spark returning to her voice, "…a trip to the continent might be in order. Now that, what did they call it? The Napoleonic business is done with. France might remember how to be charming now."

That coaxed a proper smile out of him. "You'll scandalise Paris inside a month," he said dryly.

"Of course," she replied, eyes glinting again.

She touched his arm and murmured, almost too low to hear. "Ruthless," she murmured, her shoulders drawing up. "Just like your father."

"No," Elias replied. "Worse, I fear."

Her laugh followed her as she swept toward the door.

Elias let himself think of Florence and of the strange, impossible weight of wanting everyone to find whatever happiness they were hunting.

21

Chapter Twenty-One

Elias remembered the last Bonfire Night he'd spent in Rookhaven. He'd been ten, excited for the blaze, and the fireworks his father had promised they'd light together from the back field. He'd waited by the east windows all afternoon, coat buttoned, boots polished, proof that he could be more than a disappointment.

A messenger had arrived before dusk: *Baron Blackstone sends his regrets. Parliamentary matters keep him in Town.* Elias had stared at the letter for a long time, as though reading it again might change the words.

He watched the bonfire crackle high on the moor. His mother had murmured the usual phrases—*duty, responsibility, the demands of Parliament*—but she hadn't looked surprised. All Elias remembered was the dark between the fireworks, and the quiet realisation that he'd stopped expecting his father to arrive long before the messenger knocked.

Now, years later, the village green was alight with paper lanterns and the soft roar of laughter. The scent of roast chestnuts, damp wool, and Maud's famous treacle toffee lingered in the air. Children dashed about with painted masks, music trickled from a string trio under a tented awning, and the firewood was stacked high at the centre of it all.

Elias stood near the edge, with a battered tankard of cider, watching Florence make her way through the crowd with effortless poise. Her coat was deep green, wool-lined and pinned at the throat. She stopped to speak to an older couple by the raffle table, then to two mill boys still dusted with lint.

He barely noticed the man standing beside her until Florence turned to greet him.

Layton.

The same Layton who'd bowed out of supper, and Elias had *deliberately* replaced at her table. And now here he was, beside Florence, grinning like a man who'd made a decision.

"Ah, Lord Blackstone," said a familiar voice beside him. "Excellent timing."

Mrs Fairfax, the apothecary's wife and reigning queen of Rookhaven's social committee, beamed up at him—cheeks pink with enthusiasm and brandy. "We're about to start the judging for the lanterns," she chirped. "Miss Ashcroft, Mr Layton, and Miss Wrenthorpe have agreed to assist. "We hoped you'd join them. You've made quite the impression, Lord Blackstone, especially after that generous contribution for the bonfire wood and fireworks. Thought it time you lent your eye to village matters."

Elias's gaze snapped toward Florence, her eyes narrowing when she saw him. Beside her, Layton adjusted his cravat with infuriating mildness.

If Mrs Fairfax had summoned him, his scandal was dead. Or dying. A pity Layton hadn't gone with it.

He offered a thin, practised smile. "Delighted."

Elias inspected a neat row of flickering paper shapes lit from within: stars, foxes, windmills, and something that might have been a sheep or a teapot.

Florence stood at the far end, engaged in quiet conversation with Layton, her posture relaxed. Layton gestured toward one of the lanterns, he said something Elias couldn't hear. Whatever it was, she laughed.

His gaze locked on Layton. He should have been gone. Apparently, some pests required more than one dismissal.

"I daresay the squirrel merits commendation for its aspiration," Honoria remarked beside him, gesturing toward a sagging construction of sticks, waxed scraps, and hopeful string.

Elias gave a distracted grunt. "It's not a squirrel."

"Oh no?"

"It has antlers."

"Perhaps it's symbolic. The plight of the Yorkshire bachelor—all effort, no execution."

He didn't laugh. Florence had the full weight of his attention; she had leaned in to examine a lantern shaped like a wheelbarrow, Layton's shoulder perilously close to hers.

"At this rate, you'll crush that tankard into a teacup," Honoria murmured, gaze fixed on the display. "It's strange, how Mr Layton reappeared after such an abrupt change of plans. Florence isn't naïve. She recognises sabotage when it lands in her lap."

She glanced at him from the corner of her eye. "Though this one was at least more dignified than poor Mr Farleigh. The pigeon ruse was a touch theatrical."

Still, Elias didn't speak.

"I had resolved to remain silent," she added, smoothing an

invisible crease from her glove.

He turned his head, enough to meet her gaze.

"Sometimes," Honoria added, voice quieter, "what looks like indifference… isn't."

Elias arched a brow. "No?"

She hesitated. "No. Sometimes it's fear of wanting too much—of what it might cost."

The noise swelled behind them, but between them, it stayed quiet.

"She grew up with a ghost, you know." Honoria's eyes found Florence. "And a man hollowed out by grief. That kind of loss leaves its mark."

Elias followed her gaze.

"She doesn't trust herself around you. That's what terrifies her." Honoria didn't wait for a response; she disappeared into the crowd, lantern light trailing behind her like a warning.

The weight of her words settled like a cannonball in his chest. *It was what he represented*—want that led to touch, touch that led to love, and love that demanded her life be wagered. And no matter how carefully he kissed her, how gently he held her, he would never be a safe choice. He exhaled slowly, the cold air biting at his throat.

A cheer went up. The first flames of the bonfire caught, licking skyward. The crowd surged toward it like a tide. Elias stayed back, letting the swell pass him.

He saw Florence near the carts and stalls, half in shadow, her head bowed close to her father's. Ashcroft was slumped on a bench, the stiff pride in his posture losing ground to fatigue. Florence had one hand on his shoulder and the other bracing a cane as she helped him stand. Elias stepped forward.

"You shouldn't have come," she was murmuring.

"I can't live out the rest of my days like a ghost in the parlour," her father rasped. "I enjoyed it. Even an hour out... I enjoyed it."

Her mouth pressed into a line. "You could've told me. I'd have planned—"

"I didn't want planning. I wanted to feel alive."

"May I?" Elias interrupted, already offering his arm.

Both Ashcrofts turned. The elder gave a nod of weary approval. Together, they helped him into the waiting carriage, half-shielded by hawthorn and the rise of a stone wall. The driver climbed up, and the wheels turned.

They watched the bonfire from the shadows, firelight gilding their edges.

"I want to marry you," Elias said, before she had a chance to retreat behind her mask.

She blinked. "Have you lost your mind?"

"I want to marry you," he repeated, voice steady. "Not because I've lost my mind, though that's entirely possible, but because you kissed me back. And because I lose all sense every time you enter a room—because I understand you."

"No," she cut in, sharp and certain. "You think you do. But you don't."

"I know what you're afraid of," he pressed. "I know you believe marrying me means losing control of your body, your work, your future. But it doesn't have to."

"You'll tire of it, of me," she said, shaking her head.

"Then I'll be tired and married. To you."

Her gaze sliced across him, cool and unflinching. "You're a man. You'll want—" Her voice faltered. Her gaze flicked skyward, to the fireworks exploding in bursts of crimson and gold.

He leaned in, "I want *you*, not children. Not heirs. Not some perfect household to parade through London."

Her breath hitched.

"I'll honour every boundary you set, no expectations. Not even a shared bedroom, if that's what you want."

She looked away, but not before he saw the flicker of longing.

"You wouldn't last a month," she said, voice tight.

He smiled, a dangerous thing hidden behind civility. "Then I'll spend every day proving you wrong."

She turned, fury barely veiled, striding toward the green as if distance could smother doubt.

He followed and caught her wrist. "Allow me to try."

She turned, chin lifted. "No," she hissed. "*You* try me."

She kissed him like a war cry. Desperate, defiant, and hungry. Her hand clutched his cravat, her other pressed to his chest like she could steady the thundering inside him.

He groaned—raw, cracked—and kissed her back with the force of every suppressed word, every breathless moment. His hands found her waist and held her like salvation.

She tore away first, breathless. "See?" she whispered. "That's why you'd never keep your promise."

He stared at her and gave a broken laugh. "You kissed *me.*"

"I found it *necessary* to illustrate my point."

His mouth curved, hungry and wrecked. "Well, congratulations. You've ruined me."

She shoved at his chest. He let her go. "Don't follow me," she snapped, turning away.

"Florence—" He caught her arm again.

She spun on him. "What? I said, leave me." Her breath hitched. "You should go back to the bonfire," she added, retreating a step.

"Not without you," he said—and closed the space she'd tried to reclaim.

She glared up at him, cheeks flushed from the cold and the sharp burn of her temper. "You're impossible."

"So I've been told," he said, lips twitching as though this were the most fascinating game he'd ever played. The glint in his eyes darkened. His gaze dropped to her mouth—and lingered.

A breath passed. She didn't move. Neither did he, until the distance between them became unbearable.

His mouth claimed hers with a growl that didn't sound remotely civilised; there wasn't even a pretence of restraint. Only raw and consuming heat. His hands gripped her as he pulled her with him, deeper into shadow, until her back hit the ivy-clad wall. Her fingers tangled in his hair, pulling him closer, until he could feel every inch of her pressed against him. His hand slid beneath her coat, found the soft edge of her hip beneath wool and whalebone. No silk tonight. Just the sturdy clasp of a dress meant for Yorkshire wind. And still, she trembled. He traced lower, fingers slipping under her skirts, warm and sure, like he had every right to touch her there—to claim even the air between her legs as his. She gasped—a raw, helpless sound—he caught it with his mouth, kissing her deeper, desperate to make her come apart in his hands.

"Miss Ashcroft?" The voice crashed into them like a stone through glass.

She jolted back as though burned, hands shoving him hard. He let her go, chest heaving, his heart still caught in the moment.

She wasn't looking at him. Elias turned. Layton stood at the edge of the wall, framed by firelight, the flicker of disbelief etched across his face. "I was told—" he began, voice thick with betrayal. "Miss Wrenthorpe said you were helping your father into the carriage—"

Florence's hand flew to her mouth. A sound escaped—half-sob, half-curse.

Layton's gaze snapped to Elias, narrowing with realisation.

Elias straightened, pulling his coat closed with deliberate, lethal calm. "She was."

Layton looked like he'd swallowed a nail. "And what, you followed her into the shadows like some—"

"Like a man who loves her," Elias cut in sharply.

Florence let out a hiss of air. "Don't," she whispered.

Layton's eyes darted to her flushed cheeks, the parted mouth that had tasted Elias like sin.

"Did you plan this?" she spat, eyes wild.

"If I had," Elias said, unflinching, "do you think I'd have waited so damned long?"

She looked at him like she might slap him. Instead, she spun—coat flaring, rage written in every step—and stalked back toward the fire.

Layton lingered a moment longer. Fury, shame, wounded pride—none of it quite enough to make him dangerous. He looked at Elias and said tightly, "You'll answer for this."

He raised an eyebrow. "Then make yourself useful and fetch Reverend Ward."

Elias Blackstone—Lord of the Ruined Evening—leaned against the cool stone, and watched Layton retreat.

Florence Ashcroft would be his wife. Not by vow or victory, but by scandal, and Elias found he didn't regret a thing.

22

Chapter Twenty-Two

Florence slammed the parlour door so hard the panes rattled.

The fire still crackled behind her eyelids—his hands, her breathless gasp, and the way the world had tilted when it all fell apart. "He ruined me," she said.

Honoria jolted upright on the chaise. "You're not ruined—"

"Yes, I am," Florence snapped, voice trembling. "Do you know what my father said? That I *must* marry him."

Her bodice felt like a cage. Her temples throbbed. She hadn't slept. Not a minute. "Do you understand what that means, Honoria? *Do you?*"

Honoria rose, hesitant. "Florence—"

"No. Don't you dare." Florence's eyes blazed as she crossed the room, skirts sweeping like wrath incarnate. "Don't stand there, wide-eyed and innocent. You sent Layton after me."

Honoria's expression faltered. "I told him where you might be, yes. You'd disappeared and your father—"

"Needed me." Florence's breath hitched. "And Lord Blackstone helped me get him to the carriage."

Honoria hesitated. "I saw… You looked… Free. For once. Not calculating, not resisting, or carrying everyone's expectations on your back. Just you. And him. And a moment that wasn't strangled by your careful planning."

Something behind Florence's eyes splintered. "You knew what it would *mean*. Mr Layton, seeing us—telling others—"

"I was trying to help, I saw you building a prison for yourself, Florence, and I was desperate to give you a key, even if I had to smash the lock."

Florence turned her back, one hand pressed to her temple as a bitter, broken laugh slipped out. "You betrayed me." Her voice crumbled, each syllable heavy with the sorrow of lost trust, echoing in the space between them. Florence's shoulders shook, not with sobs, but with the effort of staying upright. "You and him both."

Honoria flinched. "I didn't—Florence." Silence hung between them.

Florence crossed to the window like something inside her had snapped—like she couldn't bear to breathe the same air. "You've trapped me, Honoria. Into everything I've fought to escape. Marriage. Dependence. A future I didn't choose. And you did it, smiling at me like I could trust you."

Honoria stepped back, her gaze damp. "But you've chosen fear, Florence. Repeatedly. Maybe I wanted you to see what it feels like to choose *wanting* instead."

Florence winced, eyes glittering with pain. "When we were girls," she said quietly, "you used to braid my hair and swear you'd never lie to me."

Honoria's breath caught.

"That girl held every secret I ever had," Florence whispered. "And now you feel like a stranger wearing her face."

* * *

Florence stood by the window. Her tears had dried, but the paths they'd carved down her cheeks still burned. She felt hollow. Scraped clean. As though someone had taken a chisel to her ribcage and carved out everything she'd once believed safe. She had built this life, a fortress of industry, intellect, and unshakable independence. Her hands had laid every stone with care. And in a single night, it had crumbled.

The door opened behind her. She didn't turn.

"I told him you didn't wish to be disturbed, miss," came the maid's nervous murmur.

A voice answered—deep, assured, immovable as iron. "She'll want to see me."

"I don't," Florence said flatly.

The door closed. Quiet footsteps followed. She watched his dark reflection take shape in the glass, tall, and infuriatingly composed, as though nothing in the world had shifted.

"I spoke with your father," Elias said.

"Of course you did." Her voice was clipped, each syllable honed to cut. "Why consult me? I'm only the pawn in this arrangement, after all."

He didn't flinch. "He asked if I would do right by you."

Florence turned, her gaze blazing. "And what did you say?"

"I told him yes."

Her hands curled into fists. "And what, precisely, does doing right entail? Claiming a woman as your property to preserve her precious *virtue*?"

His eyes darkened, but he didn't raise his voice. "No. That decision was already made," he said, stepping closer, his tone low and absolute. "The moment you pulled me in to you, behind that wall—" his gaze locked on hers, steady and scorching "—and all but begged me to ruin you."

The words hit her like a slap. Florence's breath caught, humiliated, and furious. "Well, future husband of mine—" she stepped forward, her tone cutting, "allow me one final decision."

He waited.

"This marriage," she said, the words bitter on her tongue, "will be exactly what I intended from the beginning. In name only. Nothing more."

Was it rage or pain that flickered behind his eyes? Whatever it was, it passed quickly.

"We'll see," he said.

Her laugh was dry, brittle as ash. "You'll find I'm rather hard to sway, Lord Blackstone."

"I'm counting on it," he murmured. A smile ghosted across his mouth, he turned toward the door, moving with the infuriating calm of a man who *already believed he'd won.*

"I'll speak to the Reverend," he whispered. "The banns will be read. You'll be my wife by months end."

He left her standing in the fractured stillness, a trail of peat and brandy lingering in his wake. Her pulse thundered in her ears.

She didn't cry, simply stood, awaiting orders she had no intention of obeying.

* * *

Elias sat in the darkened study, drink untouched. The fire was low, spitting weak embers into the grate. The heavy silence wrapped around him. He had done the right thing. Hadn't he? So why did it feel like he'd lost something he couldn't name?

The door creaked open. "You look like a man in need of confession," said Reverend Ward, stepping inside with the kind of quiet assurance that came from being welcome everywhere.

"I need a drink," Elias muttered. "Will you take one, Reverend?"

Ward lowered himself into a chair, his brows lifted. "I'd heard the village green hosted more than a bonfire last night."

Ward accepted the glass Elias held out to him.

"It wasn't Mr Layton who said it, but the boy looked like someone had stepped on his future. I've been a Reverend long enough to recognise the face of a man who's lost something he thought was his."

Elias cracked a humourless smile. "She hates me."

Ward studied him. "She fears you."

Elias snorted. "That's worse."

"She fears what you represent," Ward said mildly. "Intimacy. Surrender. Loss, even."

"She thinks I'll take everything from her."

The reverend's gaze didn't waver. "Will you?"

Elias looked back at the fire. "I don't want to take anything. I want to give her everything. But she can't see that."

Ward steepled his fingers, thoughtful. "She's been taught that love always costs. And dearly. That belief sits heavy on her shoulders."

Elias glanced at him, curious. "Didn't realise you doubled as a philosopher, Reverend."

"I've worn a few hats in my time."

Elias leaned back in his chair, brandy swirling in his glass.

"Speaking of hats, have you ever worn one with a regiment's crest?"

That earned him an unreadable smile. "An odd question from a man on the verge of matrimony."

"I had a conversation recently," Elias said, tone measured. "With a Mr Webb."

Ward didn't blink. Didn't frown. He simply ceased smiling. "Ah," he said, as if Elias had mentioned a long-dead horse. "Yes. Webb."

"He spoke of a countryman," Elias continued, "someone… reformed. Steady hands, formerly quite handy with a blade."

Ward's eyes dropped to the fire. He watched it with the kind of stillness that says: I know exactly what you're asking, and I won't answer.

"War puts blades in all our hands," he said eventually. "Some learn to put them down. Others keep swinging, even when there's no enemy left."

Elias studied him. But Ward only blinked slowly, like a man who'd lived too long with questions and had buried most of the answers.

Then, lightly, he added, "Webb hasn't been seen in a while, has he? Not since… before the village bonfire? Curious, that."

Elias gave nothing away.

Ward glanced at him. "I do find it interesting, the way men vanish in this part of the world. Not in body, but in invitation. One minute, they're everywhere. The next? Not so much as a whiff of their cologne on a dance card."

He stood, smoothing his cassock with slow fingers. "I'll read your banns on Sunday. Three weeks from now, she'll be yours."

Elias rose too, arching a brow. "No sermon on temperance or responsibility?"

Ward smiled faintly. “Keep your sword sharp, my lord. But remember—not every battle requires one.”

He stepped out, silent and swift, like someone used to slipping through shadows. Elias watched the door long after it had closed, and thought of men who knew too much, and said far too little.

23

Chapter Twenty-Three

The church bells echoed off the frost-tipped stones as Florence emerged into the crisp November air, her chin high, pulling on her fur-lined gloves with a force that betrayed her inner turmoil.

The congregation had shifted like a stirred beehive the moment Reverend Ward read the names—hers and Elias's—aloud. No outcry. Just a collective intake of breath, a rustle of heads turning, whispers pressed behind gloved hands. The kind of silence that wasn't empty, but loud with judgment.

Reverend Ward's sermon still clung to the damp air. She hadn't heard most of it, not over the roar in her ears and the weight of Elias's gaze boring into her back through the entire service.

And there was Honoria—two pews over, all wide eyes and remorse, as though *she* dared to be hurt by Florence's silence.

Florence gripped her pelisse so tightly the stitching groaned.

Elias waited at the church steps, one hand resting on his cane, though he hardly needed it. He inclined his head as she approached—galling, infuriatingly polite—she could feel the heat in her chest rise.

"Miss Ashcroft," he said, stepping into her path.

"Lord Blackstone," she replied, all honey and knives.

"A word, please," he said, his tone leaving no room for argument.

"I've heard enough from you."

He kept pace, undeterred. "You've yet to listen," he said, voice low.

She froze mid-stride to the carriage. "I don't require your assurances or your assistance—" Her voice faltered as she caught sight of Honoria, who had edged closer, her presence a silent plea to speak. Florence's chest burned. She hadn't spoken a word to Honoria since learning it was she who'd confided her fears to Elias—Honoria, who had seen to it that the kiss at the Prendhurst bonfire was witnessed and spread like wildfire.

Florence fixed her with a stare, blistering like a furnace and offering no hint of forgiveness.

Honoria stopped in her tracks, colour rising to her cheeks. Still, she managed a hesitant, quiet, "Florence—"

Florence held up a gloved hand—a single, imperious gesture—and turned back to Elias. Her glare fixed him in place as she spoke in a low, vicious voice, startling a few nearby parishioners. "I don't need you to rescue me from a mess *you* helped create."

He stilled, his fingers flexing with a telltale twitch. She didn't give him a chance to reply. She turned on her heel and swept toward the waiting carriage. "Home, and make haste," she barked, climbing in.

"Yes, miss." The driver shut the door behind her with a startled thud.

She could still feel their eyes on her as the wheels lurched into motion, Elias's steady, infuriating calm and Honoria's wounded pride trailing after her like an icy wind that found every seam.

As they left the village, the driver pulled the horses back, cautious on the silver-slick road.

"Miss, it's bad going," he called over his shoulder. "We'd best take it slow—"

"Faster," she bit out.

"Begging your pardon, miss, but it's not safe—"

"I said *faster*."

He obeyed. She felt the lurch as the pace quickened, the wheels slipping now and then on the frostbitten lane. The trees blurred past, black against a sky the colour of old ash. Her anger swelled with every jolt and bounce of the carriage, filling her throat, her lungs, her very bones. How *dare* they. Both of them conspiring, deciding what was best for her, as though she were a child to be shepherded toward her own happiness.

How *dare* they believe they knew her better than she knew herself?

Her thoughts vanished as something caught beneath them—a rock, a rut—followed by a crack that echoed through the axles, the carriage tilting violently to the side. The horses panicked, the driver shouted and fought for control, but it was too late.

The carriage buckled, Florence was flung forward, the air ripped from her chest. The metallic tang of fear filled her mouth as her head struck the frame. Pain. Cold. Screaming wood.

And then—

Nothing.

* * *

Elias lingered after Florence disappeared, fading into the brittle November air. Nearby, Honoria twisted her cloak, her gaze lost in the distant haze. He glanced at her sidelong. "She'll come around," he said, a thread of doubt lacing his words despite his attempt at reassurance.

A short, tense sigh escaped Honoria's lips. "You think so?"

"Indeed," he replied simply.

She shook her head, eyes gleaming with a mix of regret and defiance. "I thought…" Her voice faltered. "I thought if she could see you for what you are, she'd stop being so afraid."

Elias's mouth ticked. "And what am I, exactly?"

Honoria looked at him, a soft, rueful smile gracing her lips. "Perfect for her. Too perfect, maybe."

He inclined his head toward her. "Thank you," he murmured. "For what you did. Whatever she says, I know you meant it well."

Honoria gave a curt nod, swallowing whatever else she might have said.

Elias turned, bidding Reverend Ward a polite farewell with a promise to see him "next Saturday, God willing," and descended the steps to where his horse waited.

By the time he mounted, the weak sun was a fading memory behind thick grey clouds, and the road glimmered with frost, promising a cold ride. For the first stretch, he rode at a measured pace, his mind full of Florence's words, her glare, and the cruel twist of her mouth when she'd accused him of creating the very mess he was trying to untangle.

The memory lingered, heavily, but his hands held steady on

the reins, tuned to the horse's subtle shifts beneath him. The road to Mooredge twisted on, colder with each turn, the wind clawing at his coat and howling in his ears.

As the next bend revealed itself, something caught his eye. A carriage. Tilted at an unnatural angle. As he drew closer, His stomach dropped. Florence.

One wheel was gone, splintered. The whole thing sagged into the ditch. The horses screamed, eyes rolling, hooves kicking at nothing. The driver was down, blood streaming from his face as he scrabbled at the door.

Elias dismounted before his horse stopped. "What happened?" he barked.

"She's trapped, my lord," the driver gasped, his hands slick and shaking. "We hit the ice—it tipped us. She's not—she hasn't moved."

The words barely registered. Elias was already at the door, peering through the cracked glass.

Florence lay slumped with her bonnet askew, a streak of blood at her temple, her body crumpled and unnaturally still where she'd been thrown.

"Hellfire," Elias spat, a chill snaking down his spine. The door wouldn't budge. He stepped back, teeth clenched, snatching a rock from the dirt. "Stand back," he said curtly. He brought the rock down against the window—once, twice—until the glass shattered and fell away. He reached in, bracing himself on the frame as he slid his arms under her.

She felt warm but frighteningly limp, her head lolling against his shoulder. "Easy, love."

When he straightened, the driver was staring at him, his face ghostly pale and his eyes wide with shock. Elias jerked his chin toward the saddle. "You'll have to steady her legs when

I mount," he said. "We need to mind her head; she's already taken a knock."

With a nod, the driver steadied the horse, while Elias, one arm still firmly around Florence, used his strength to swing up into the saddle. He settled her across his lap, her head cradled against him.

"Free the horses," Elias snapped. "Ride to the village and fetch the doctor. Tell him to come to Mooredge immediately." The orders left his mouth with military precision, but his pulse was a hammer in his throat. Fear—raw, ungovernable—surged through him, a sensation he hadn't tasted in years.

* * *

The clock struck midnight. Elias barely noticed. He'd worn a line into the rug, back and forth, again and again, his hands clasped behind him. It had been two days since the accident, and still she lay abed.

Tom had brought a tray some hours earlier—untouched now, the tea cold, the bread stiff. The valet had hovered longer than usual, as if expecting instructions that didn't exist. Elias suspected the poor boy's valeting manual hadn't covered *what to do when one's master's intended lies unconscious upstairs*. Eventually, Tom had retreated, murmuring something about stoking the fire.

The doctor had arrived each morning, delivering the same cool reassurance: nothing grave. A bruised head and a body too battered to do anything but sleep. It would pass, though he'd added with a knowing look that she ought not to be moved yet.

Elias had nodded, mute, and resumed pacing.

Lady Cheverley drifted into the drawing-room like moonlight in mauve silk. She lowered herself into a chair with practised elegance. "You're making the house dizzy, darling," she said, a faint smile on her lips as she watched him complete another pass.

"She hasn't woken," he muttered, dragging a hand through his hair.

"She stirred this morning," his mother reminded him. "Called you stubborn. Frankly, an excellent sign."

He stopped, one hand braced against the mantle, eyes fixed on the low, flailing embers. "I should have gone after her."

Lady Cheverley tilted her head. "You can't be everywhere at once. And she's safe. That's what matters."

He exhaled through his nose, unconvinced.

The floorboard above creaked, no doubt a maid checking on her. His shoulders tensed at the sound.

His mother's hand touched his sleeve. "She will be fine, now sit before you frighten the servants."

"Her father?" he asked gruffly, ignoring the chair she gestured toward.

"Worried sick," she said, with a sigh. "The man can't walk outside without coughing up a lung. I sent word that she's being looked after. He trusts you."

Elias's jaw shifted at that, though he said nothing.

"And for propriety's sake," his mother added airily, "I shall remain in attendance, of course. You're quite welcome."

He shot her an exasperated look, but the corner of his mouth betrayed him, softening just enough.

24

Chapter Twenty-four

The third morning dawned grey and bleak. He stood at the window with a cup of cold coffee in his hand, watching frost crawl across the drive. Lady Cheverley had retired hours ago, after insisting again that he at least try to lie down. But the thought of Florence, pale and still, made rest impossible.

Maud had brought him breakfast at dawn, set it down with a clatter and muttered, "She's made o' tougher stuff than you think, m'lord. Yorkshire lasses don't fade easy."

He didn't answer her; he stared at the plate until the eggs cooled and the toast dried. But the words had stayed with him—gruff, unsentimental, and somehow more comforting than anything the doctor had said.

He was about to resume his habitual pacing when carriage wheels disturbed the quiet. Frowning, Elias set the cup down and moved to the door. By the time he stepped outside, the carriage had stopped, and the door swung open.

Out stepped a fur-wrapped, pink-cheeked Honoria Wrenthorpe. Her chin lifted with the defiance of a woman who *would not be turned away*. She looked like a duchess-in-training. And also unmistakably like a friend prepared to fight.

"Miss Wrenthorpe," Elias said, inclining his head.

"Lord Blackstone," she replied, sweeping past him toward the steps.

A footman scrambled to take her cloak as she entered the house without waiting for permission.

Elias arched a brow but made no protest. She was the first visitor besides the doctor, and frankly, he wasn't inclined to send her away.

"To what do I owe the pleasure?" He asked, trailing her into the drawing room.

Honoria turned on him, keen-eyed and indignant. "You know why I'm here. Don't pretend otherwise. She's not your wife yet. And I've held my tongue for two days, sat at home while everyone gossiped. I must see her."

Elias watched her, this small, and unusually bold creature glaring up at him as though she had every right. The corner of his mouth twitched into a smile. "I wouldn't dream of stopping you," he murmured.

That startled her, though she covered it with a sniff. "No? I thought you might lecture me on propriety and appearances."

"I've more pressing concerns than appearances."

She glanced at him, and her gaze softened. "You haven't slept."

"No."

Silence stretched, quiet and weighty.

"Well," she said, squaring her shoulders as though frightened by her sympathy, "I should like to go up now. If you'll allow it."

Elias inclined his head toward the stairs. "By all means, my lady. Perhaps she'll wake for you."

Honoria paused, eyes searching his face. And in that instant, Elias let himself admit how grateful he was that she'd come at all. "Thank you," he said, surprising them both.

* * *

Florence stirred to the sound of a familiar, insistent voice. Something cool and damp brushed her lips. She flinched away with a groan.

"Oh, stop wriggling, you ridiculous creature," came Honoria's unmistakable voice, adept as ever, but with something else wound into it. Worry, maybe. Or fear.

"You've caused quite enough fuss already."

Pain bloomed at the base of Florence's skull, a steady, pulsing throb. And the light—even through her closed lids—was too bright.

"You're awake, aren't you?" Honoria pressed.

Florence felt the faint tug of a comb sliding through her tangled hair.

"You can stop pretending now. Trust you to try and escape your nuptials this dramatically. Honestly—"

Florence cracked one eye open and squinted at her friend. "You're loud," she croaked.

Honoria froze; a strangled laugh escaped that quickly dissolved into a sob. "Oh, thank God," she breathed, setting the comb down and pressing her fingers to her eyes.

Florence sighed weakly. "And dramatic? You created this mess, you know."

Honoria let out a long breath, her face creasing into a contrite frown as she perched on the bed.

"I know," she said softly. "And I am sorry. I thought—truly—I thought you'd thank me. Eventually."

That startled a faint laugh out of Florence. "You are impossible."

"You're no better," Honoria said, though there was no heat behind it.

A quiet moment passed between them, the kind two lifelong friends could manage without needing to fill it.

Florence's voice came quietly, almost to herself: "I envy you sometimes. Having both your parents. Overbearing as they are, at least they care enough to meddle."

Honoria gave a soft huff. "Looks can be deceiving. It's all for show and propriety. They care about appearances. Not me." She leaned forward, elbows on her knees, voice gentler now. "You, on the other hand, you've got a father who adores you. Who actually raised you. Let's be honest, he lets you get away with murder. You run a mill empire, Florence. Few ladies can say the same."

Florence let her eyes flutter shut, let the words settle. For so long, she'd believed she could live like her father had—self-contained, untouched by love, invulnerable. But lying here, bruised and exhausted, she saw that path clearly for the first time. It didn't look like strength anymore. It looked like loneliness. She didn't want to end her days in some vast, quiet house, buried in ledgers and silence, trying to prove to the world that she'd survived it all alone. She wanted more.

She wanted Elias. The thought landed with a quiet inevitability, like snow settling on the moor.

Honoria glanced at her. "He loves you, you know. Desperately. He hasn't slept. Won't leave the house. Looks like death warmed over, and I'd be smug about it, if he weren't so noble about hiding it from everyone else."

Florence turned her head and met her friend's gaze.

"So," Honoria said, "what are you waiting for?"

Florence took a slow, deliberate breath and let herself admit it. "Nothing," she whispered. "Not anymore."

* * *

A flushed maid found him in the corridor. "She's wakened, m'lord," she said breathlessly, eyes bright. "Proper this time."

Elias's stomach clenched, hope and fear twisting together like twine. He forced himself to nod. "Thank you." He stood for a moment, fists curling and uncurling at his sides, letting the stillness settle. Letting the ladies say whatever needed saying before he shattered their peace by barging in like a man who'd spent two nights on fire with worry.

And then he couldn't wait a moment longer. He half-ran to the door and pushed it open without ceremony.

The scene inside was almost comical. Honoria perched at the edge of the bed, back to the door, mid-laugh. Florence sat propped against her pillows, pale but present, dark hair loose about her shoulders. Her lips were parted, as if caught between a scolding and a smile.

They both turned at his boots on the floorboards.

Honoria's eyes sparked with mischief. She stood, smoothed her skirts, turned to him with all the sweetness of a debutante and none of the innocence. "Lord Blackstone," she said, too sweetly.

"Miss Wrenthorpe."

"I daresay I've already overstayed my welcome," she added,

voice full of theatre as she swept past him toward the door. "I shall leave you to it."

Elias stared.

Her eyes danced. She shot Florence a look that made his ears burn, then glided out, humming to herself all the way down the stairs.

As he crossed to the bed, Florence looked up at him, eyes clear but tired, her voice a rasp of warmth. "You look dreadful."

"You're one to speak," he murmured back, though his chest loosened just hearing her tease him.

He sank into the chair beside her. She tried to sit straighter and winced.

"Don't," he said at once, rising to steady her. "Stop moving for God's sake. Florence, must you make everything a battle?"

Her fingers closed around his hand.

He stilled.

"Elias," She swallowed

Something in him broke apart at the sound of his name on her lips. "Yes?"

"I'm not sure I'll be able to stand at our wedding," she said, voice low, mouth curving. "Might we postpone it a week? Long enough for me to say my vows without falling over."

He blinked. "Pardon?"

"Besides," she added, eyes glinting now, "wrinkling my very expensive wedding gown would be a tragedy."

He gaped at her. "You've changed your mind."

She nodded. "I don't want to live like my father. Or like Honoria's parents. I thought I could—but I can't. I want…"

She hesitated, then met his gaze, steady and unflinching. "I want you. And I think—no, I know—we could have a marriage unlike any before us. Something entirely ours."

He was stunned into silence. "You've hit your head harder than I thought," he said at last, lips quirking despite himself. "I should fetch the doctor."

She tightened her grip on his hand. "Don't you dare," she breathed. "Kiss me instead."

He laughed, disbelieving. "You must be gravely ill," he teased, but leaned in, brushing his lips over hers, slow and tender, his thumb grazing her cheek as she sighed into him.

When they parted, she wore a quiet, secret sort of smile, and it almost destroyed him.

"How long," she murmured, "might I stay at Mooredge without scandal?"

He gave a low chuckle, pressing his forehead to hers, their hands still tangled together in the coverlet. "That depends," he murmured, his voice rough. "If you promise to be mine forever and marry me the moment, you can stand—you need never leave at all."

"Never?" she whispered, her lips grazing his cheek.

"Not for a single day."

She relaxed into him. "And if I *don't* promise?"

He pulled back enough to meet her gaze, knowing exactly what she'd see—hunger held tight at the edges, and a gentleness he'd never given to anyone else. "I'm used to scandal, Florence. I'll weather every gossip Yorkshire can throw at me if it means keeping you here. At my side. Convincing you of my love until my dying breath, if I must."

She laughed—a breathless, shaky little sound. Without breaking his gaze, she lifted his hand and pressed her lips to it. "You've already convinced me, Elias Blackstone," she breathed. "I love you. Even if you are insufferable."

His throat tightened. He brushed her temple with his lips,

a kiss as soft and reverent as a prayer. "Good," he murmured against her skin, his hand cradling her cheek. "Because I've loved you since the moment you looked me in the eye and told me you didn't need me. And I've been proving you wrong ever since."

Her breath hitched, and she closed her eyes. "Don't stop," she said.

"I won't," he vowed.

He kissed her brow, then stayed there, breath mingling with hers, letting the silence fill with everything he didn't need to say. For once, there was no need to move. No need to chase or retreat. He was exactly where he was meant to be.

He was finally home.

The End.

Epilogue

Whitby, March 1815.

The cottage was quiet but for the faint hiss of the sea and the occasional creak of the old bed beneath them. Florence lay sprawled on her stomach across the feather mattress, sheets tangled at her hips, the air faintly warm with salt and Elias's cologne.

"If you keep staring at me like that," she murmured into her folded arms, "you'll wear holes right through me."

From beside her, Elias made a low, appreciative noise. His hand rested lazily against her back, thumb moving in slow, possessive strokes, as though to say: *mine.*

"If you think a look is the worst you'll endure today," he drawled, "you've learned nothing in three months of marriage."

She huffed, eyes still closed. "Mm. And yet here I am, alive despite your wicked intentions. Reverend Ward would be shocked."

"Reverend Ward," Elias drawled, rolling onto his side, "gave a sermon that sounded suspiciously like a dare—something about love being found in unlikely places, about patience and the slow bloom of affection." Elias murmured, brushing her shoulder with his mouth, "I'm not saying Reverend Ward meant it as permission, but that sermon had more temptation than scripture. And I intend to honour it. Thoroughly."

She cracked one eye open and gave him a sly smile. "He was right, though. It *did* bloom—with thorns."

"You're the thorn."

"And you're the brute who plucked me."

He laughed low, the sound dark and fond all at once, leaning down to capture her mouth. She melted into it, languid and warm, before shifting with a stretch, the sheet whispering as she moved.

When she swung her legs toward the edge of the bed, Elias caught her by the waist and hauled her back against his chest.

"And where," he demanded, his lips at her ear, "do you think you're going?"

"I promised to write to Honoria," she said primly, though it came out more breathless than intended.

"It can wait until you can walk without wobbling."

She wriggled free. He groaned and flopped onto his back, releasing her with a dramatic sigh.

Ignoring his muttered protests, she made her way to the small writing desk tucked beneath the window.

"She says," Florence called over her shoulder as she uncapped the inkpot, "that her mama is twice as determined this season. Apparently, they've paraded her in front of every titled man between London and Inverness, and not a single one will do."

"Shocking," Elias muttered, unrepentant as he watched the sheet slide lower down her back.

Florence threw him a warning look but carried on. "I was thinking," she ventured, "we might invite her here. For the last fortnight of our stay."

His head snapped up. "Here? *To Whitby?*"

"Yes, Elias, here. To *Whitby*."

"In our *cottage?*"

"Where else would she stay—the stables?"

He propped himself up, glaring at her with mock betrayal. "This is our honeymoon."

"It's March. We've been married since December."

"And yet I'm still not done with you."

"You're *never* done with me," she said, with a smile that made him grumble.

She dipped her quill, then paused, quieter now. "Without Honoria, we might not have married at all."

He gave a small, rueful smile. "I would've found a way."

"You're impossibly arrogant."

"And you love me anyway."

She glanced at him, heart warm, then abandoned the letter. Returning to the bed, she took his hand in both of hers and pressed a kiss to his knuckles. "Yes," she said. "More than I ever meant to."

His throat bobbed with the effort not to react, though she saw right through him. He cupped her cheek, his voice rough with feeling. "Good. Because you're mine, Florence Blackstone. Every inch of you. And if I have to endure a dozen more transgressions to keep you at my side, so be it."

She laughed and tucked herself into the curve of his body. After a moment, she asked, "Shall I write to Honoria?"

"If you must."

"I must *rescue* her, love."

"Fine," he sighed, drawing her tighter to him. "But she stays in the guest room *furthest* from ours. And if she sets so much as a slipper in this room—she's on the next coach back to London."

Florence smiled into his shoulder, unrepentant. "We'll see about that. Heaven help you if you think you're in charge."

Elias groaned, but didn't argue. Instead, he kissed her hair and let her stay curled there, warm and laughing, as the sea whispered outside and their bargain unfurled with the tide.

Afterword

Thank you for reading The Blackstone Bargain. If you've made it this far, you have my deepest gratitude and possibly a fondness for brooding lords, stubborn heroines, and Yorkshire grit. This story began as a daydream, written late at night between work, parenting, and trying to keep the cats off my keyboard. It's my debut novel, and I poured everything I love about historical romance into it: slow-burn tension, class clashes, emotional restraint, and love that arrives when you least want it (but most need it). The journey doesn't end here. The Northern Grit & Gowns Saga continues, with more tangled love stories set against the backdrop of Regency Yorkshire. You'll see some familiar faces and meet new ones who are just as impossible to ignore. A Small

Request from Your Humble Author

If this tale brought you even half as much enjoyment as Elias and Florence brought each other vexation, would you be so good as to leave a review?

It needn't be a sonnet (unless you're feeling poetic); a few lines will do. Your words help other readers find the story and keep authors like me in tea, ink, and questionable historical research. If you'd like to stay in touch, get sneak peeks of upcoming books, or receive exclusive extras, you can join my newsletter: https://preview.mailerlite.io/preview/1660103/sites/159726152041104772/VLKnight

Until next time,

V.L. Knight

About the Author

V L Knight grew up in Yorkshire and still counts it among her favourite places in the world—from the windswept moors and rolling dales to the rugged coast and its hidden second-hand bookshops. Her love of historical romance began young and never quite let go.

She lives in the UK with her two teenage children, four cats (so far), and an ever-growing collection of unread books. By day, she works full-time as a nurse. By night—and in whatever stolen moments she can claim—she writes love stories laced with longing, sharp dialogue, and the grit of Northern England.

Though she always dreamed of writing a novel, it wasn't until her forties that she finally found the courage to put the words on the page.

The Blackstone Bargain is her debut novel.

If you enjoyed The Blackstone Bargain, I'd love to hear from you. You can find me on:

Instagram: @vl_knight_author
TikTok: @vl.knight.author
Facebook: V L Knight - Author
Goodreads: https://www.goodreads.com/vlknight

Come for the brooding lords. Stay for the book recs, bonus content, and chaos (usually involving cats and caffeine.)

Subscribe to my newsletter:

✉ https://preview.mailerlite.io/preview/1660103/sites/159726152041104772/VLKnight

Also by V L Knight

A sweeping Regency romance series set in the wild heart of Yorkshire, where moorland winds meet industrial grit and love never arrives politely.

Each book weaves together sharp heroines, brooding lords, and simmering tension—amid mill towns, crumbling manors, and scandalous supper parties.

Stand-alone love stories. Recurring characters. One unforgettable county.

The Blackstone Bargain

A disgraced noble. A fiercely independent woman. In Regency Yorkshire, love is the most dangerous bargain of all.

Honour's Worth (Coming early 2026) Whitby, March 1815.

The sea is wild, the winds merciless—and Lady Honoria Wrenthrope is determined to escape her mother's latest campaign to see her wed.

Invited for a quiet fortnight by her dearest friend, Florence Blackstone, Honoria expects sea air, polite company, and a temporary reprieve from titled suitors.

She does not expect Dominic Vauclain.

A half-English, half-French privateer with smuggler's hands and a gaze like stormlight, Dominic is the estranged son of a nobleman and half-brother to a Scottish laird; he's a man who's spent his life dodging expectations—and debts.

She's meant for London ballrooms. He's sworn off anything with silk gloves and a pedigree.

But the tides have other ideas.

Printed in Dunstable, United Kingdom

67661121R00119